CW00850810

BEGAT

Tales of Disappointment

Philip Skotte

This is a work of fiction. All of the characters, names, incidents, organizations, and dialogue in this novel are either the products of the author's imagination or are used fictitiously.

LifeRich Publishing is a registered trademark of
The Reader's Digest Association, Inc.

LifeRich Publishing books may be ordered
through booksellers or by contacting:

LifeRich Publishing
1663 Liberty Drive
Bloomington, IN 47403
www.liferichpublishing.com
844-686-9607

ISBN: 978-1-4897-3058-9 (sc)
ISBN: 978-1-4897-3057-2 (hc)
ISBN: 978-1-4897-3059-6 (e)

Library of Congress Control Number: 2020916619

Print information available on the last page.

LifeRich Publishing rev. date: 09/22/2020

CONTENTS

DEDICATION

To Maribeth with thanks
Love of my life
Mother of our children

INTRODUCTION

It was plague time and our lives were filled with disappointment. Careers, cafes, commutes and other comforts fled away. We locked ourselves in our homes, feared strangers, disinfected packages that came to our door. We did not expect this in our time on earth.

In our time.

That was our reference point and all that we knew. The ancestors' voices were stilled.

We lived now.

On earth.

Earth was our home. The only place we had. Heaven was a distant thought. A fantasy,

like death,

unlikely.

The plague shook our complacency about our time on earth. It turned our thoughts inward, backward, forward. Made us doubt our sureties. A few of us did not survive this new disease.

We wondered if those dead went to another place. We spared a thought for a place other than earth and a time different from now.

Some of us had journeyed onward, died.

If you have time, this is their story.

Or at least a little part of their story. This is about one single person they met over there, one person among many.

It may be worth your time because she is a most important guide.

When your time comes,
and it will,
you will meet her too.

It may surprise you that she is a carpet weaver, and that she will lead you backward.

Her name is Sarai.

SARAI

Sarai lives in heaven's desert.

Heaven's desert has a beauty all its own. Travelers can see further, even to a far horizon, views unblocked by trees. The ancient geology of creation is bared, multicolored rock layers and millennia of sculpted erosion unveiled. A dry place focusses the mind and strips away distractions.

In heaven's desert there is an oasis called Al Amin where travelers stop for water and rest. At the oasis are cool springs, date palms, fruit trees, spare but adequate provisions and warm hospitality.

This is where travelers meet Sarai and other carpet weavers. These have been weaving for centuries and are the storytellers and historians of antiquity. Some of their carpets have been in the making for millennia; others have been set aside awaiting the arrival of new travelers. When a carpet is finished, there is a great celebration before it is loaded onto the back of a camel for delivery to another place.

Each carpet begins its life as a story. A traveler in the oasis, over tea and date cakes, remembers aloud from the other side. The dry desert helps the speaker to the point, to get his or her fingers around the knot. The teller's brow often furrows with concentration and perhaps the memory of pain.

Sarai, a Turkic speaker from the old Silk Road, has been listening and weaving for ages. Most of her completed carpets comfort people far away in towns, cities or roadhouses. She threads as she hears; knots as she understands. For many a traveler, Sarai's finished carpet makes clear the incomprehensible, creating sense from disparate threads. Some carpets are woven from various stories, over generations, across time. Once she pulled an unfinished carpet off the shelf after a century, when a new traveler referenced a thread of it. His story helped complete the carpet and tied it together, making something beautiful and complete from pieces.

Sometimes, the purpose is clear, even if it is near the end of one's life. "What you intended for evil, God meant for good," said Joseph.

Joseph, his brothers, father and family understood the threads of slavery, injustice, betrayal and lies—yet also saw them woven into the saving of many lives.

More often, a person passes over with threads still scattered. It is Sarai's purpose to weave them together with the benefit of heaven - sight. For the people in Sarai's tent, drinking tea and telling their stories, the weaving makes clear that even before they left the other shore, they had been here. Their deeds and the deeds done unto them, good and bad, are retold. Blood red threads through darker colors run, golden weaves cross knots of trial. On the oasis in Sarai's tent, heaven works backwards in time.

Sarai had been a Central Asian nomad before the writing of books. Mostly, her people survived on scarcity—a few grazing animals, occasional game, birds, wild berries and grain. Her people were few on the dry steppe and frequent death kept them so. When they met other bands, it was a guess if they were friend or foe. If not foe, they would stay together a while and trade stories.

Stories.

Before the writing of books, there were words. If you

survived to adulthood and had an ear to hear, you listened, retold, remembered. No one was honored more than a good teller of tales. Around the firelight, under the stars, in a foot- and hoof-trampled space between endless waving grasses, you listened.

By the time of her passing, Sarai was a library. Her stories were catalogued by author, subject and genre. She was a genealogist; she knew who came from whom. She was a comforter; she made sense of pain and confusion. She was a theologian; she found God in story, before all stories and after them.

If she had not been mute, she would have had much to say, and been a keen teller of tales. But never having uttered a sensible word, she wove her library, genealogy, comfort and theology into carpets. For Sarai, a carpet was more than art. A carpet was life.

Now with voice to speak and sing, she does both with the joy of one denied such pleasures for so long. And yet she has not lost the acuity of ear, keenness of insight and skill of weave acquired on the other side. In fact, these old skills are sharpened here. Honed even more is the ear for God's voice heard long ago on the noiseless steppe.

It happens now and then that, after many stories over generations and with her rare insight, the threads still cannot not be turned to beauty and completion. When the gifts God has given her are insufficient for the telling, God himself speaks in her ear: Pull this thread over that one; dye this wool a deeper red; this knot untie.

Our ancestors have been coming to Sarai's tent for millennia. They sit, pull their legs up under themselves and lean forward. Sarai gives them tea and goes to the back room. She returns, sometimes hours later, with an unfinished carpet and lays it on her loom. Our forebears reach out and rub the wool between their fingers. Its knotted wool is strangely familiar.

Long before this present plague, an old Swede with one eye, crossed the desert on camelback and arrived at Al Amin in the cool of evening. He was on his way to the Great City, but travelers had told him to visit Sarai first.

The morning he first arrived at Sarai's tent, he pulled the flap aside and bowed as he entered. After removing his shoes, he presented Sarai with bread and olive paste from the market.

John Malcolm sat on a carpet before the loom and looked at Sarai with his one good eye.

"I do not know where to begin," he said tentatively.

It was often this way at the first meeting. Sarai reached across and took John Malcolm's calloused hands in hers. "Tell me when you were born and where, and how you died."

"I was born on a farm called Flahult in the year 1887, one of seven children. I died full of years in Minneapolis. They buried me of old age with my wife and daughter."

SARAI

THE IMMIGRANT

John Malcolm was born when Sweden was poor and before the iron triangle of sex, babies and marriage had been broken by the modern wonder of birth control. In 1887 many Swedish couples had large families and lived on small farms. There were too many Swedes for those farms to feed. Stories about the New World, the money to be made and the open land, roiled the conservative tranquility of the Swedish countryside.

Many a farmhouse dinner turned to the young leaving. A letter from a neighbor was read. Mother rose from the table and went to the kitchen. She busied herself with the clean-up, dried tears with an apron. So many left Sweden, and they did not come back.

A mother loves her son. Loves her daughters too, of course, but a son more. Especially when there is only one son among seven children. The son of her love was also the future of Flahult, for those were the days of primogeniture. The first-born son took the entire farm, bringing to it his wife who would bear their grandchildren. John Malcolm and his wife would move into the red painted working house and his parents to the house for the old ones. Every Swedish farm had the two houses, just so. The old ones would watch the grandchildren and do what they could. Their declining years were spent helping the family scrape by.

Scrape by. Those were the words they used for Falhult, a farm that never produced enough in the best of times. Rocky, small, mostly forested. Worse still, the family did not even own the farm. They had it year upon year by promise from the Church of Sweden, in exchange for minding the graves of a childless Parson and his wife. Keep the grave clean in perpetuity, and you may work this farm for a small rent.

John Malcolm went to school, worked on the farm, fought over girls at the dance barn, bought a bicycle that he used to escape his many sisters. He saw his parents' thankless struggle in the fields, heard the letters from America, turned things over in his mind. When he reached draft age, he went to the Army.

"That is where I knew my strength," said John. "I was bigger and stronger than the other recruits and they made me an officer. I was proud of my manhood and stood tall with my chest out."

Sarai poured another cup of tea and smiled at the thought. She had heard this before, usually from men. Men are strong. They bear the weight of protecting the village, the dangers of the hunt. They endure pain without tears, sorrows without weakness. A real man can be counted on for courage in battle, to brave the icy wind, to trim the sails in gale force winds.

It is no small thing to be a man.

"And so I decided to immigrate. At the age of 24, I said good-bye to my parents and sisters gathered in front of the farmhouse. It was not our way to cry or hug, but we felt it strongly. My father shook my hand and wished me well. I promised to return with money to improve the farm."

Sarai had by now readied a carpet on her loom and gathered threads between her fingers.

"And how did this immigration go for you?" she asked.

"I was strong. The first year I loaded and unloaded goods

in a train yard. I toiled 364 days straight without stop. I knew how to work. At night I went to school to learn English. I met a Swedish girl named Emilie and asked her to marry me. She said yes."

"Then I switched to a construction job and learned to mix and apply plaster. That is where I had my accident."

"Ah yes," said Sarai, "you lost your eye."

"They sewed it shut after the accident. I asked Emilie if she still wanted to marry me. Again, she said yes.

I could bear the loss of an eye. Even a limb. If I had lost a leg, I would have borne up, been strong, carried on without bitterness. I was a man. I was not weak."

"Then why," asked Sarai, "are you here?"

"I am here, not for my eye, but for my daughter."

JOHN MALCOLM

GLORIA

As a mother loves her son, so a father loves his daughter. John Malcolm and Emilie bore three children, one a daughter. John was not a religious man, but once when he held his infant daughter he gazed upon her ear, the tiny curls, intricately fashioned folds. It came upon him, a thought unbidden, that this ear could be no accident, that a Creator had designed this wonder.

And he was thankful.

As she fell off to sleep in his arms, he watched her. A strong man. He would have given his life for her. Both eyes. Every limb.

She grew awkwardly, as all girls do, through her infancy and into her teens.

And finally, it was clear, she would be a beautiful woman.

The two sons went off to war, one in the Navy and the other in the Army. They fought the fascists and the militarists in a righteous crusade. Gloria wanted to do her part.

But by now she had developed an illness, a thing of the colon, not well understood, but dangerous.

Sometimes it was worse and sometimes better. She lost weight, gained it back. Her parents did all they could, listened to doctors, nursed and loved their daughter, encouraged hope. Even took her to church.

Gloria confided to her diary a hope to move to San Diego if only the doctor would let her. As John Malcolm had heard of America by letters, Gloria heard about San Diego from her brothers. It was a place of palm trees and sun, sandy beaches and tan sailors. If any place could improve her health, surely San Diego was that city.

Finally, the doctor felt it was safe. John Malcolm and Emilie took Gloria to the Minneapolis train station and waved as the train inched forward. Perhaps all would be well after all.

Sarai stood and walked past John to the tent opening. She stepped outside without a word. Already knowing the end of the story, she wanted to gather herself. She knew that she had much work to do, that to weave this carpet would require every ounce of her love and genius. She thought about the older carpets in the storeroom and wondered how many of them would be required.

After standing in the desert sun to warm her face, she turned back to the tent, brushed the fold aside and motioned for John Malcolm to join her outside.

As they stood together, she pointed to the eastern hills.

"After you leave here, you will travel onward to a place called the Forum, a rendezvous for the resurrected. There you will meet your daughter and many others that you love.

But you already know that.

Death has already lost its sting and the grave its victory.

No, you are here because, after you buried Gloria, you lived another 42 years. You want to talk about those years, to understand why you were not strong, what you missed, what could have been.

John Malcolm, I must go back many generations, show you our oldest carpets, tell you ancient stories. This will be our work for many days. And then you will go forward.

Come back tomorrow. I will show you an ancient weave from when life was simple. Before ships, doctors, farms and wars. From nearer the beginning, when the emptiness will tell us much about ourselves and the way of the Maker.

I will bring forth the oldest carpet I have.

It is from Africa.

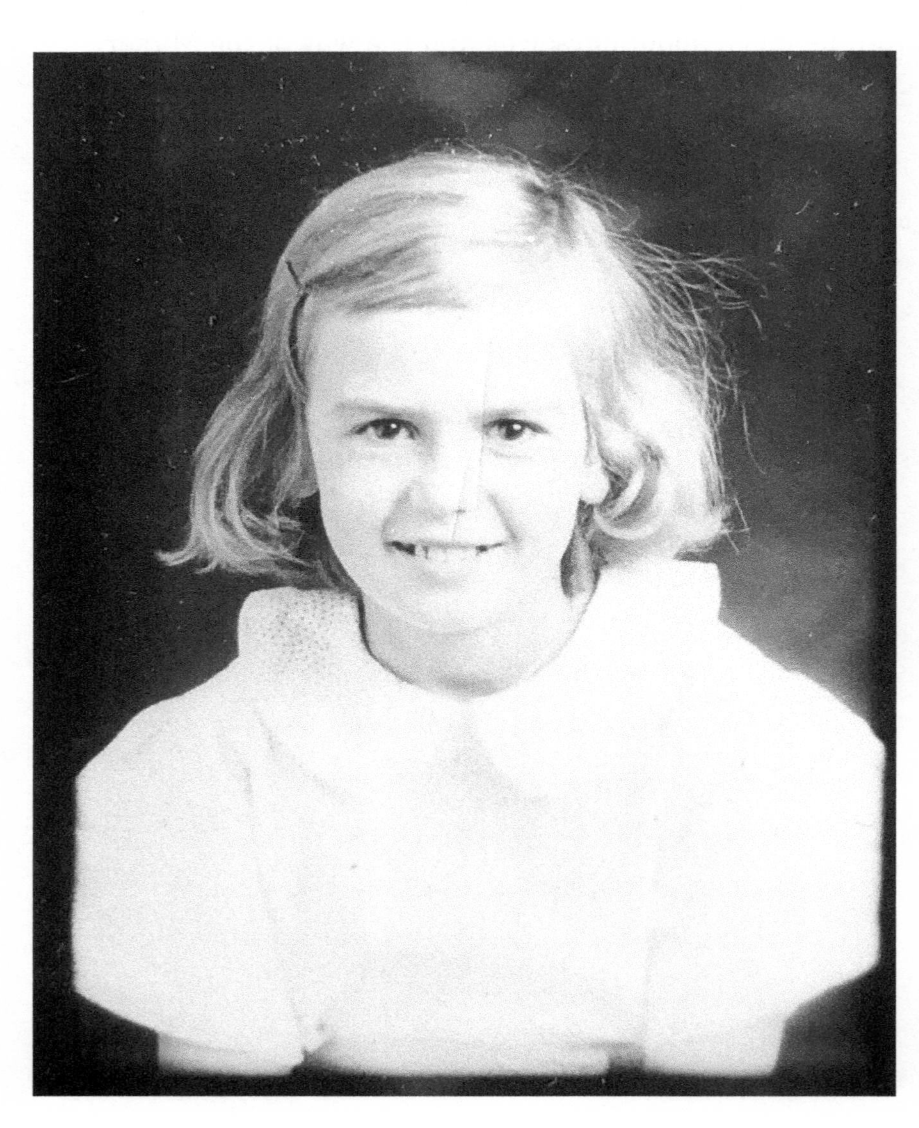

GLORIA

THE AFRICAN

In a place now called Eritrea, a small band of twenty humans followed the animals that they hunted. The women collected nuts, berries, insects. When they reached the shore, they discovered other things to eat, living creatures in shells, insects that lived beneath the sand and left tiny tracks to ease their finding.

The old ones, keepers of fire, were at hand to light dry wood for warmth and to blacken the meats from sea and grassland. Their world was warm, the sun overhead beat down all day. They told stories from the ancestors about a place where the sun lived longer, but in these days the sun shortened its life for a time, before growing large again.

The band walked along the shore for many days, without aim or purpose, other than to find food, tell stories around firelight, mate and raise their few young. As they walked, they kept the shore and the rising sun on the side of their arrow arms.

Sometimes they fought with each other, over food, an insult, a partner or unfair sharing when food was scarce.

"How little things have changed," Sarai thought. She laughed as she ran her hand over the ancient worn threads.

There was oil from other hands blackening this first edge of the oldest carpet.

"Touch it," she told John Malcom.

When he hesitated, she took his hand and pressed it against the blackened wool.

"Oil preserves this wool. The oldest weaves need human touch to stay fresh and supple. Your oil will mix with that of thousands over millennia and keep this carpet alive."

She closed her eyes as their four hands pressed against the fibers. "Over and over this story has been told and from it springs many others. The Maker wants you to know the story of Adda, the leader of this band. Like you, he was a strong man.

On this better shore, he has traveled farther up and further in, and you will meet him one day. At your meeting, remember to him how his story was the first you heard in Sarai's tent.

Adda was like you, stronger than the others. He had two good eyes and his arrow eye was keen to target. He brought home food, grew into a decisive leader, settled arguments. He had two women, more than his share. The younger men in the band eyed Adda jealously. That was the way then. The young men had to wait.

Adda's oldest wife had born him many children, but only one survived. That boy child, dark with the sun, begat other children, who in turn begat yet more. One of them crossed a shallow sea many years after, and from that one you are begotten.

But I am getting ahead of myself. Where was I?"

John reminded her, "You said Adda had two wives. You said he was strong like I was strong."

"Adda was muscular, but like all on that side, he grew weaker as he grew older. And as he grew old, so too did his wives. The sun wrinkled their skin and earth's weight stooped their bodies. Adda's body also weakened, but not his eye.

There was a young girl, more comely to look upon than the rest, who began to blossom. Her name was Yar. Her skin was smooth, her eyes sparkled with energy. Under her spare coverings, the curves of womanhood were unmistakable. Adda began to position himself near her on the trek, to seat himself beside her at the fire. Once he shared with her a piece of rabbit leg. Adda thought on Yar when he slept, could feel the warmth of her body, smell her sweat.

At times he was overcome with desire.

Adda's distraction was noticed by the band. His wives laughed nervously with each other. Young men stiffened, lest the rare prize of Yar go to one already old, who had already known women and begotten children. Yar herself was unsure. It was an honor to be desired by Adda and yet others were more vigorous.

One night as the band settled under the night sky, Adda decided to move to Yar. Heart beating with anticipation and sweat breaking out on his temples, he rose from between his wives and crept toward Yar's place. He would crawl under the skin covers to her side.

He moved out of the fire's light, circled to the far edge where Yar lay. As he neared her place, he heard sounds that made his heart stop. Low murmurs and whispers, the power of a female and a male together.

Confused, Adda paused. Then he circled back and lay himself in his place, with his wives. They had heard him rise in the darkness and knew his purpose.

Why am I telling you this story, John Malcom? What does the story of Adda and Yar have to do with the 42 years you lived on earth after your daughter died?"

"I do not know. In truth, I do not know. But it is a good story and old too."

"John Malcolm, I am telling you this story because Adda

never lay with Yar. He never had his wish. He died on that shore and was buried in a cave barely eight months after that night. Yar went to a younger man."

John Malcolm cleared his throat. "I only had one wife, Emilie. Not two. And I never even chased another woman."

"But you did desire them. Or at least the thought entered your mind. And what did you do? You denied your desire. You turned again unto Emilie and for this you are praised. But there is more to this story than your faithfulness to Emilie.

The Maker's world was a place where we did not get all that we desired. Partners, longer life, better health, more respect, wealth, power. And John Malcolm, even the health of our loved ones. We lived with unmet desires, we denied ourselves, and finally we died unsated.

John Malcolm, disappointment was built into that world."

John Malcolm leaned back into the cushion and closed his single eye.

Sarai stood and moved the carpet further up the loom, revealing a lighter patch.

"Desire on that side was complicated. Adda's desire conflicted with other desires, those of his wives, the younger men and even that of Yar herself. Perhaps his desire for Yar even conflicted with his own desires.

One of the younger men who wanted Yar was Adda's son Cana. In fact, as Adda learned in the next days, it was Cana who had been with Yar that night.

Touch this carpet again, John Malcolm. Feel Adda's sadness in it. Go to the edge and find a new thread. That is the granddaughter of Adda, born to Cana and Yar. That one is your forebear.

Adda and his first wife begat Cana. Cana and Yar begat Seth. Seth begat yet more. And there were many generations."

"I hope you will not be angry," said John Malcom, "but Adda's story does not answer the death of my daughter. Nor even the loss of my eye."

Sarai topped up their two tea glasses and laughed.

"I know," she said, "But I like this story because it is old and simple and is like many others. And the Maker, for some reason, wanted you to hear it.

You will never again experience disappointment. Disappointment was built into the other world.

On this side our desires are ordered differently. Here you will know longings of great beauty and anticipations of intense power. These longings will be in harmony with the desires of others, with your own desires and with those of the Maker. These yearnings will be stronger than any on earth. Every single one will be sated, and beyond all expectation.

That is why this is called heaven. This is the first of my stories."

"This is the oldest story I have ever heard," said John. "May I return again tomorrow for another?"

Sarai, pulled another carpet forward, a little lighter, less oiled, but clearly old.

"This one is thousands of years younger than Adda's, still well before your time. Your people continued north following the retreat of the ice. They lived in caves, hunted cats and mammoths. They knew one another and begat offspring.

Feel this empty space in the wool. You can almost put your finger through the warp. This is a story that will interest you. It is about a man in a cave called Agtelek in a place later called Hungary. We will start at his end, as he lay dying."

THE CAVEMAN

Ruk lay on his left side and listened to the trickle of water inches from his face. It was quiet, cool and dark in the cave, three conditions for the best sleep. That is why he had asked them to lay him here.

The light at the cave opening glimmered beyond his feet, and he felt the approach of steps. It would be his granddaughter, the one who always came in the mornings.

She felt his forehead in the cool darkness and knelt beside him.

"Do you want food this morning father?" she asked.

He rolled unto his back to relieve the ache in his shoulder and sighed.

"The Great Spirit still has not come for me. I am waiting."

He reached for the bowl of cool water and she helped him to sit up. Drinking deeply, he stared toward the light at the cave's opening.

"What have you brought today, daughter? Besides the food, what have you brought?"

"I have brought your fire starters for the next world. If it is cold there, you can use these stones for fire to warm yourself. What else will you need?"

Ruk thought back on his life and the things he had used.

He had hunted with bow, arrow and club, kept warm with furs, sewed skins with bone and sinew and started fires. As he grew older, he kept fire smoldering in a pit when the younger ones went to find food. The Great Spirit had already come for his wife and others in his clan.

"Lay my things beside me and I will use them in the next place. Bring the others tonight and build a fire in this room. Draw my hunts on the wall and sing our songs. And then I will sleep the long sleep. It is time. The Great Spirit is near."

Sarai paused in her telling and looked at John Malcolm. The tent was quiet except for their breathing and light wind on the fabric.

"Imagine cave's stillness with Ruk on his left side facing the sound of water. He had lived his life well; fed his people; begotten children; been kind to friend and fierce to enemy. When he weakened and heard the Great Spirit, his people stopped their trek at that cave. They laid him on his side, watched over him, gave him his needs for the next world. This night they would sing, mark the walls and remember his doings.

His granddaughter stayed near him all that morning as his breathing grew shallow. When the sun reached the sky roof, she was relieved by another. That night the whole clan came into the room and bid Ruk a good journey. They drew his knees up to his chest, cleaned him lovingly with water and closed his eyes in sleep. Toward morning, they left the cave and piled rocks over the entrance."

Sarai stopped the story and the tent was again quiet.

"I told you about Ruk's end, but I want to tell you something more. His people left Ruk's things next to him because they knew he would rise again. On the other side, we all knew that, even ancient people knew it. Death was with us but so was life.

You always knew your daughter would die, just not when

she would die. If she had died after you, that would have been a happiness.

Before she left at noon, Ruk told his granddaughter that he was happy. She asked him why. He told her he was happy because his son and his granddaughter were still alive and that he could die before them. And he was happy to die and live again to meet the other ones who had gone before."

John Malcolm shifted uncomfortably and stretched his legs.

"Yes, of course my daughter would have died. But I did not want to see it. It was an untimely death. A daughter should not die before her father."

"Ruk's story cannot take away your lament. It lasted for 42 years. That is why there is a hole in the carpet, where you can place your finger. Because your lamentation was true."

"But you gave yourself over to something besides lamentation.

It was anger.

The anger was not lament. God wanted to suffer with you, to share in your grief, but you pushed Him away.

And you pushed Emilie away. And your sons. You went cold."

"And that is why I am here," said John Malcolm, "to understand the 42 years where I might have done otherwise."

Sarai swirled her tea and gazed across the cup's rim at John Malcolm. "You have come near the truth. You are here, not to understand how you might have *done* otherwise, rather you are here to understand how you might have *been* otherwise.

Your daughter awaits you, better than ever you remember her. From this side, your 42-year absence from her will seem short. But the grief and lamentation you knew was real. The Creator does not deny that.

The Creator is not like the Thor of your far ancestors, the

one with a hammer. No, the Creator is the one of your nearer ancestors, the one on the cross.

If you visit Agtelek, you will find Ruk's room. His hunts are on the walls. Smoke stains on the cave ceilings. Human remains are scattered with the things they needed hereafter. And if you are quiet, very quiet, you can still hear the water's trickle. This trickle is the sound of the Great Spirit's tears, the Creator's sorrow."

"Thank you for this story," said John Malcolm, one cheek wet with tears. He started to leave, but then turned back to Sarai and the carpet laying on her loom.

"May I once more feel the hole in that carpet, the place where thread runs out?"

John Malcom felt the gap, the place where there was no thread, the emptiness. He rubbed the woolen edges tenderly between his fingers. Then wiping his wet cheek with his hand, he placed his fingers just there, in the place of lamentation.

THE WITCH

When John Malcolm returned the next morning, Sarai was outside the tent picking Basil and Thyme from her herb garden. Her basket full of greens and lavenders, Sarai rose to greet her guest.

"Try this," she said handing John Malcolm a sprig of fresh Basil.

"All manner of herbs grow here and some, like this Basil, can be added to our teas and breads. On the other side we had Basil too, but not as delicious or subtle as this."

John chewed the Basil appreciatively and asked if the herbs on this side were good for healing.

"Oh yes, and more than on the other side. After you leave here, you will enter a forest called Gilead and meet a man named Yaw. He knows the ointments and salves from the trees and fauna. Forest herbs are the strongest for healing.

The story I will tell you today is about a woman from the old world. She lived about eight hundred years before your time. She was expert on the herbs of your country, a forest healer. She survived many illnesses and childbirths into old age and was respected in her village. They called her the old woman of the sacred hill, but her given name was Freya, after Thor's wife.

You can probably guess that she lived before your country had churches and before your people were baptized. She practiced healing before Sweden had clinics, doctors or 'real' medicine."

Sarai led the way, with her full basket, into the tent. After seeing John Malcolm to his cushions, she walked to the steaming kettle and poured two cups of tea, into which she dropped fresh sprigs of Thyme and Basil.

After handing a cup and saucer to John, she pulled a carpet from the shadows and spread it on the floor where she and John could both see and touch it.

"Ruk, from yesterday's story, begat a son, who begat the granddaughter who watched over Ruk in his last days in the cave. When she came of age, that granddaughter, begat two children. One of her two children joined a band that ventured further north. Eventually, those people arrived in Sweden, crossing a frozen Baltic Sea in hard winter. Those became your people and populated your land.

Far from the sun of Adda and Ruk, their skin, eyes and hair lightened and they became fair. After many generations, Freya was born with waxen hair and blue eyes. After a manner, she is your mother."

Sarai ran a hand over the carpet to a place of green and red.

"You can see here the green forest and the red fire.

Freya was strong like you. She survived illnesses that killed others and childbirths that laid mothers low. She listened to older ones who knew the herbs of the forest and the salves, potions and ointments which could be made from them.

As you know, some of this knowledge was useful. There were oils that healed. And of course, there were brews that harmed.

With her knowledge of herbs also came the old religion. Freya could call on spirits, unknown powers and even the dead. She sacrificed to the gods when villagers needed assistance, especially when plague or famine threatened. She gathered the elders and brought the victim forward, usually a small animal, occasionally a cow or horse. Rarely a human.

This was why Freya was called a Witch."

John Malcolm was interested in this story. It was closer to his home than the older stories and it was about a time he had heard about, when Sweden was Pagan and pre-Christian.

"Did they really sacrifice humans?" he asked with incredulity.

Sarai, pointed to a spot in the carpet that was blood red.

"Every single society in the old world sacrificed something. It was universal across our species. Sometimes it was vegetable, more often animal and occasionally human.

In Freya's entire lifetime she only offered two human sacrifices, at desperate times, both to the high gods, Odin and Thor.

When you lived, Odin and Thor were distant memories, but the days Wednesday and Thursday are named after these gods to remind you from whence your people came. These were gods of power. Thor, best known of the two, had his hammer and used it to throw thunder across the cosmos. His wife Freya, after which your ancestors named the day Friday, ruled part of the underworld and took to herself half of those slain in battle. Odin ruled the other part of the underworld, named Valhalla, where he feted the other half of the battle slain.

You will notice that these old gods had to do with power, hammers, battles and thunder. Freya sacrificed to them to get their attention and to curry their favor."

John Malcolm bent over the carpet to better see the red colors running through the green woven forest.

"Perhaps it is better that this old religion passed away," he said, "especially if they sacrificed humans."

"Every religion has truth in it, John Malcolm, but the religion of your ancestors also had a fault.

A few weeks after Freya offered her second and last human sacrifice, a thought came to her mind. She did not doubt the power of her gods, but the reluctance of the sacrificial victim, the pleading on her face, marked Freya's conscience. Mother Freya had wanted to save the child, to love her even. And yet, the gods had demanded knife and blood.

The gods were strong, but were they love?

Freya died before the new religion came to Sweden, but she dared to question the gods out loud and told the elders she would make no more sacrifices like that of little Lilla.

Had she been alive when the black-robed friar brought the cross and the story of God Himself being our sacrifice she would have gladly embraced the teaching."

John Malcolm looked at Sarai thoughtfully and asked if the old religion had left other traces than just the days of the week.

"John Malcolm, old religions always leave traces. Even after Jesus' cross replaced Thor's hammer, hundreds of years later, there were Swedes who doubted the love of God. They still thought God was Thor and they were angry at him. They did not feel the gentle scarred hand on their shoulder, the hand of comfort from the one who had suffered with and for them."

John turned his face away from Sarai and looked down at the dregs in his teacup.

"You are speaking of me," he said, "and my anger."

"Yes," said Sarai, "that is why the Creator gave you this story."

FREYA

THE SABBATH DAY

In heaven, every seventh day is the Lord's Sabbath, a day of rest and gladness, different from other days.

Early on the Sabbath, John Malcolm awoke and walked to the café on the corner. The café owner, a Nigerian, knew the oasis of Al Amin well. He offered John suggestions on how to spend his day. He could join a congregation for worship, walk along the desert's edge or row a boat on the Oasis' small pond.

John decided to take a walk and, at days end, relax on the pond. The Nigerian packed him fresh bread and cheese for an afternoon meal.

"Where are you from?" asked the Nigerian, as he handed John his boxed lunch.

John replied that he was from Sweden but had immigrated to Minnesota as a young man.

The Nigerian thought for a moment and then pointed to a nearby table.

"That man is also from Minnesota and arrived several years before you. His name is Ingve Karlson."

The Nigerian led John to the table, introduced the two men and then went back to his work behind the bar.

As people do when they meet a townmate far from home,

the two began to ask each other questions. Where did you live? Who are your parents? Do you know so and so?

As often happens, they quickly found common ground. Ingve had been a math teacher at a nearby school and had heard of John's children.

"There were so many children and not enough time. I will take time for each one on this side. Aida, a carpet weaver, is explaining things to me before I go forward.

This week she explained to me about 'Divine Moments.'"

"What are Divine Moments?" asked John Malcom.

"They are times when you felt God in an unusual way. I made a list of them and we traced them on my carpet. I remembered some moments and there were others that had been hidden to me until now. Aida showed me those.

Then she gave me a math problem, probably because I was a math teacher. She asked me to choose a number between zero and one hundred to describe my satisfaction with life on the other side. I chose the number 'seventy.'"

"That is not a bad number," said John.

"Sarai may not ask you the same question. You were not a math teacher.

Aida wrote my number seventy on a little board. Then she started to subtract in case a given Divine Moment had not happened. There was the car that missed me at forty. My wife's successful cancer cure. The time I almost drowned.

And on it went. The number kept getting smaller and smaller.

Finally, there was the accident on my bike on Central Avenue, North East. That almost ended it for me at the age of seven. I thought the number could not go any lower.

But then Aida told me, if my parents had not met, I would be a zero.

You should ask Sarai for a math lesson like that one John."

John shook his head and took a sip of coffee.

"I remember some of those times. The births of children. When I saw the Statue of Liberty for the first time. Once I stood to pull the starter cord on my outboard motor in the middle of Lake Lewis. The boat leapt forward and nearly toppled me into the water. That would have ended it. I suppose there were others that I did not know of."

"That was the point of Aida's lesson, John! There were so many I did not know about. I was someone's full-time job. I wanted to be at one hundred, but I was blessed to be at any number above zero!

Did you ever ask about your angels? There were messengers assigned to you. You can ask about them. Even if you don't get a math problem, you can still find out your numbers."

John Malcolm laughed.

"I am going for a walk and then for a boat ride. I will ask. And when we meet again, I will tell you."

John thanked Ingve for the math lesson and they agreed to meet again. He walked to the edge of the Oasis and started to list the Divine Moments he could remember.

There was the night in the barracks as he and Axel lay in their bunks talking about America. They spoke excitedly late into the night and finally agreed to emigrate together after they left the Army.

The construction accident that had taken one eye, could easily have taken both.

The last night of English class when he had asked Emilie if he could walk her home.

Gloria's ear.

As John walked along the palmed fringe of the desert and looked across at the expanse of sand, the Spirit of the Lord came upon him and brought another memory to his mind.

He saw himself behind the wheel of his car with Emilie in the passenger seat. Emilie was screaming and waving her hands frantically.

She was shouting in a confused mix of Swedish and

English that John, or Yon, had run a stoplight and just missed being hit by an onrushing semi-truck.

John pulled to the edge of the road and waited for Emilie to calm down. Then he continued driving silently to Mora for grocery shopping.

The memory drifted into the sand as John watched. Then, as if from the past, he saw an angel walking toward him. Although John had never seen the angel before, there was something familiar in his presence.

The angel drew near and smiled at John.

"You were a full-time job on the other side. You drove the car, but you could not see. Emilie could see but did not drive. I have no idea why you arranged it that way.

I am Pradeep. My brother angel is Anil. We trained in Mumbai, India, as traffic specialists. That is why the Lord assigned us to you. For trips to Mora, one of us could do the job.

Once it was my day off and Anil came running. 'They are going downtown, Pradeep! You must help me.' I leapt from my bed and joined Anil for the ride south. There were two close calls and much screaming. It was the last time your son allowed your grandchildren to ride with you.

There was the winter you fell down the stairs and your wife could not raise you. Anil went with Emilie to fetch an elderly neighbor through knee high snow. I calmed you and slowed your heart rate. It was not easy to be your angel, John Malcolm.

More than once Anil and I argued over whose day it was to watch you.

You exhausted us."

John Malcolm looked at Pradeep and saw that his figure was shimmering as though to disappear.

"Pradeep, before you go, I want to thank you. And thank Anil too. From the bottom of my heart."

The Spirit of the Lord led John to the pond and into the

boat. As the evening fell, he rowed slowly to the middle of the water. Stowing the oars and settling on his back, he looked up at the night sky.

The stars began to twinkle and glow in the blackness. Millions upon millions of them.

"There," said John, "is the constellation Gemini, the two brothers, my angels. I did not know they were Indian traffic specialists.

They are arguing about whose day it is to watch me. Emilie screaming, 'Yon, a train is coming!' I am driving through anyway. Anil and Pradeep are slowing the oncoming engine. Emilie is white with terror. Pradeep is shouting. Anil is laughing.

Only I am silent.

A strong Swedish man."

And then John Malcolm began to laugh. He laughed so hard that he cried, tears streaming down his cheek from the good eye. He did not stop laughing for a very long time. The stars shimmered and twinkled with mirth and gaiety. John Malcolm, the heavens and the Maker were full of merriment.

As he lay in the bottom of the boat looking up to the heavens, he raised two strong arms in thanks.

"You smiled on me more than I knew. You laughed with me, and sometimes at me too.

Oh day of joy and gladness!

This is my Sabbath."

A BAD PRIEST

John Malcolm returned to Sarai's tent refreshed from his Sabbath rest. He could see that Sarai also looked renewed and anxious to begin.

"It is good that you rested yesterday, John Malcolm, because today's work will be hard. The story I have to tell is a harrowing one that will take us to the edge of life."

John responded with a chuckle.

"Sarai, I started with hard immigration, the loss of an eye and the death of my daughter. You followed with stories about Adda's unfilled desire, the death of Ruk in a dark cave and Freya, an old woman on a sacred hill before the coming of the Gospel. Your library of carpets is a hard one and spare of laughter."

"That is true, John Malcolm," said Sarai. "At the oasis of Al Amin, the Maker finds your disappointment, loss and scars. To be whole in heaven, you must leave earth well. Today I will take you to a hard place, a time before yours. We will touch the bitter fringe of life.

The Maker wants you to have this story. After today, my stories will still be painful, but the light will grow, until at last you come to the Great City of God.

"Well then," said John, "let us begin." He settled back into the cushions and drew his legs up under himself.

"Freya begat Tiv and Tiv begat Birgit and Birgit begat Johannes. Johannes knew Molly and they bore a daughter, named Gota. During Gota's time, the village built a stone church on old Freya's sacred hill. This was often the way of the new religion. They built churches and chapels on places sacred to their pagan forebears, whether spring or hill. They called this church Breareds Kyrka. It was a beautiful place and remains to this day.

Breareds Kyrka and the village of Simlangsdalen were far from the King and the Bishop. Therefore, the local people did not always follow the edicts of state and church. That is why their priest had a wife and five children. The village looked the other way as they considered it lucky to have a priest at all in those days. As they said, "Better a bad priest, than no priest at all!"

So it was that Father Knut celebrated Mass and kept the high holy days. Everyone pretended that Ebba, his wife, was a widow and that her five children were fatherless. Father Knut, out of Christian charity, had taken the whole lot under his wing, going so far as to live with them.

Sometimes fiction is the best way to deal with an uncomfortable truth."

John Malcolm laughed. "After Luther, we gave up on celibacy and our priests could marry. Some had many children. It sounds like Father Knut was ahead of his time."

"Indeed, he was," said Sarai.

"He was a good husband to Ebba and a loving father to their five children.

You said that my stories are sad, but in between the hard chapters are many happy ones. There were days of laughter, good food, smiling faces of little ones, sun overhead, gentle wind in the trees. I do not always read you these chapters, but they are in the carpets too. And without them, life would not have gone forward. The heavy chapters do not blot those out, but our purpose here is to know the hard times and understand the other side through new eyes.

When their oldest was eleven and their youngest two, the sickness came to Simlangsdalen."

Sarai rose from her seat and fetched a small carpet from behind the stove. It was almost entirely black. She laid the carpet at John's feet and guided his hands to feel the rough unfinished wool.

"This carpet is not black because it stays near my stove. It is black because it was woven from the time of the Black Death, when eighty million Europeans became thirty million within a decade. The few living could not bury the many dead.

I will not bore you with the grief and sadness that broke the continent. The numbers are so large and the empty towns so terrifying. I will just tell you of Knut and Simlangsdalen.

Within days of the first illness, villagers were sickening and falling. Knut's wife and children were among them. Knut too had the sickness and it marked him terribly, but for some reason, he did not die like the others. One after another, his children died. His dear Ebba too.

He buried them and many others, not deep for he had not the strength for digging. Over each he said the words of the church, memorized, for he could not read. Ashes to ashes, dust to dust. In the name of the Father, and of the Son and of the Holy Ghost. Amen."

Until only he, so far as he knew, was left.

Lying in his home on his straw bed he looked up at the reed ceiling, the smell of death in the air, the languid Swedish summer sweating out its last warmth.

You never faced this John Malcolm. You never faced the death of all you knew, the end of civilization, the darkening of the world, extinction.

Knut's experience was common. Call it the harrowing, the

Holocaust, the Killing Fields, Bloodlands, the last offering. There were times, John Malcolm, when your ancestors, and many others, experienced the very edge of life and looked into a black abyss the like of which you never saw, not even when your Gloria died."

Sarai fingered the black carpet and pulled John's hand to the darkest place.

"Stay your hand here for a few terrible moments, in the place where all of life ends."

They sat in silence for a long time.

Finally, Sarai spoke.

"Imagine if Knut had been right, that the whole human race was extinct. Only he had survived, and he only for a little while longer. Imagine him carrying on alone for months or years until he saw the last sunrise and sunset and then crumpled into his boots."

"This is a dark story indeed," said John Malcolm.

"After your time, the study of the skies advanced, and astronomers determined that our Milky Way Galaxy had perhaps 400 million stars, of which our sun was one. Then they reached out further to estimate the number of galaxies in the Cosmos. The scientists said that there were at least two trillion. And among all this vastness, so far as we knew, there was only life on our tiny earth. And life only for a short time longer, before our sun burned out and all went black.

We were, all of us Knut, lying on our straw bed, looking up at the reed ceiling, the smell of death in the air, the languid Swedish summer sweating out its last warmth.

Only the distractions of life kept us from knowing it.

Touch this carpet here again, where the darkness ends."

Again, the two of them sat in silence.

"After days or hours, he knew not which, Knut rose and wandered alone to the empty path in front of his house. All around were fresh mounds where he had buried the dead. The air was full of flies for those yet untended.

Knut's face was pockmarked and much of his strength was gone. He left the village and walked out of the town. Eventually he came to a place where three people still lived, a father, a mother and their lone daughter. At first, they would not allow him near their encampment, but after a time they let him closer and finally he joined them.

The young woman, Alba, lacked a mate and months later, out of desperation, she proposed to Knut.

Knut's energy and desire were both spent. His drive to reproduce had turned to ash. He had a choice. These were the last humans on earth. He could end all future human suffering simply by declining Alba's hand. Or he could ensure future suffering and pain, by joining Alba to beget offspring. The choice was not easy, and Knut pondered it long. To exist on earth was to suffer. To end existence was to end suffering.

Knut's choice was not unlike that of the Creator at the beginning of our race, or again at the time of Noah. To create and preserve humans with choice, in a world of second causes was to introduce suffering and pain.

When God said, 'Let there be Light, and the evening and the morning were the first day,' so began our race, and later our suffering.

Our suffering and God's suffering too, for it is God's nature to suffer with us.

This was made clear on that sacred hill.

Not Freya's sacred hill in Simlangsdalen.

Rather the hill outside Jerusalem.

There God subjected Himself to our futility and entered the abyss.

Knut and Alba begat Agneta and William. William and Agneta found others who had survived and begat more generations. The suffering continued, but never again, at least in Sweden, did it reach the harrowing abyss of Knut's day. Not yet.

John, you have remained unusually silent this day. I have

given you much to think on. I take every visitor to the edge I have shown you, and I ask them to look over. You should go home and rest."

John rose from his seat and thanked Sarai for her story.

"I never went to the edge before. I never let myself," he said.

Sarai rose and opened the tent flap, letting in sunlight.

"We can go to the edge on this side because we are in heaven now and know the ending. On earth, we hid from it, lost ourselves in diversions. We did not dwell on the inevitable end of all things, the imminent destruction of our race.

Those few who looked over, either by choice or through fate of circumstance, always came back from the edge changed.

And usually in search of God."

KNUT

DISASTER AT SEA

When John arrived at Sarai's tent the next morning, she set before him a tray of fresh dates and biscuits.

"The dates are from our oasis. The biscuits are from an old Scottish recipe. You will learn that some of your people came from that land.

We have spoken of unfilled longing, death, suffering and extinction. Today I will bring you a story of failure."

John thanked Sarai for the refreshments and winked with his good eye.

"Well, this is another link in your somber chain. I look forward to more sadness and misery.

It is a good thing we are in heaven or I should be broken by now!"

Sarai laughed and excused herself. A few minutes, later she returned with a carpet of sea blue and silver, mixed with many other colors.

"In this carpet you can see the blue of the North Sea and the silver of pewter and tin. The Cross of Saint Andrew is for Scotland and scattered among the knots are castles and ports. Here is a ship and I want you to meet her captain, a man named Calum.

Calum was a Ship's Master in Medieval times when

Scotland and Scandinavia traded by sea. From Sweden he carried timber and iron. From Scotland his ship bore salt, cloth and tin. It was a profitable trade and Calum did well for his family and his crew. He was an honored merchant in his home port of Dundee, Scotland.

To be a Ship's Master in those days was to take risks. The journey from Dundee to Stockholm took four to six weeks and the sailing season lasted from April to October. Outside those months, the North Sea was treacherous and impassable.

Calum made one trip per year, enough to support his family in Dundee, pay his creditors and prosper his business.

In 1592 Calum had the idea to cut out the middlemen who raised the price of pewter and tin between Cornwall and Dundee. He decided to borrow a larger advance from his banker and sail direct to Cornwall, take on a load of tin at wholesale prices and then make for Sweden before the onset of winter storms.

He decided to gamble everything on this bold venture for two reasons. First, his wife had died, leaving him with three offspring to raise alone. And second, he felt growing weakness in his lower back that portended an end to seafaring.

Calum and his crew boarded the Lady Fife, waved to their families on the dock and hoisted sail for Cornwall, far to the south.

If not for Calum's sterling reputation as a Ship's Master, his crew would not have assented to this new and risky venture. But just in case there was any remaining doubt, Calum doubled his crew's pay."

John Malcolm took another bite of the biscuit and commented on its richness.

"This reminds me of the oats we ate in Sweden when I was young. And it has the scent of real butter and cardamom."

Sarai smiled at the thought.

"Calum was here many years ago and gave me this story. He showed me how to make the dough for these biscuits and I have been baking them ever since. He was a strong man who left his country unwillingly and settled in yours."

"How was that so?" asked John.

"It happened like this," replied Sarai.

"The Lady Fife sailed south along England's eastern shore; arrived in Cornwall as hoped; took on board tin at low price. Her crew provisioned her with kegs of fresh water and victuals, then made a course for Sweden.

By now the sailing season had grown old and the winter storms of 1592 decided to arrive early. The Lady Fife rose and fell on the North Sea. She beat herself against the wind and contrary sea. Her sails shredded. Her bulwarks heaved. The sailors exhausted themselves keeping her aright. Master Calum almost gave up pointing her bow into the huge oncoming swells. The days were fearful and the dark nights terrifying.

When Calum reckoned that they were near the Skagerrak, where the North Sea touches the Baltic, he muscled the Lady Fife to starboard. If they could make the turn, they might find shelter from the heaving North Sea.

It was unlucky that Calum had tried his venture in 1592 when Winter came early. Had he gambled on this venture in 1591 or 1593, he might have been successful. But this was a year when many ships sunk or foundered, not just the Lady Fife.

Hours after Calum turned the Lady east, the worst happened and the old sailors immediately knew their loss. The crew and Calum felt the ship lurch, not the lurch of sea and wave, but the grinding of hull against land.

Sadly, this western shore of Denmark was not one where the sea showed mercy to those who foundered. Even though the shore was sand, Lady Fife keeled to Starboard and many hands were lost in the churning waves.

Over the next hours and days, Danish villagers worked their way to the wreck, saving Calum and what crew they could. When the waters calmed, Calum returned to salvage some of the tin and pewter scattered on the shore or chest deep in the frigid sea.

Calum's gamble had failed.

After seeing his crew off in the spring, he gathered the remnants of his freight and put it aboard a coastal schooner bound for Sweden's western shore. He determined to sell what he could and send the proceeds quietly for the care of his children.

If he had returned to Dundee, he would have been thrown into a debtor's prison until the last farthing was paid or the banker took mercy.

Calum was trapped in Sweden."

"Well," said John, "there are worse places to be trapped. I hope he met with kindness there."

"He was able to sell his remaining wares in the countryside. He sent money home to relatives for his children. Best of all, he met one of your ancestors, Krista. Together they begat a child, the first whose birth appears in the official church records."

"So, we are almost in modern times," laughed John Malcolm.

"Yes, almost in modern times. Calum ended his days in the province of Haland. He never lost his foreign accent just as you never lost yours. He died with a poor back but had both his eyes until the end."

"His story was not so bad," said John Malcolm.

"He survived the shipwreck, supported his children and left offspring in Sweden. To top it off, he had me as a descendant! I am pleased to claim him as an ancestor."

Sarai moved the carpet on the loom and directed John's eye to the point where the blue sea turned to the brown and yellow of land.

"When Calum sat here with me, he did not see his life as you now see his life. He thought himself a failure. Perhaps it was because he had fallen from great wealth and esteem to lesser. When he sat where you are now, he unburdened himself to me. I showed him different carpets than those I am showing to you.

But there is one carpet I showed to him, that I will also show to you. For failures, you cannot do better than this story, woven by our Lord Himself."

Sarai reached for a carpet near the tray of biscuits on the table.

"Jesus told of a master who went on a journey and gave talents to three servants. On his return, two servants had invested their talents and doubled them. The master commended both those servants and made them rulers over many things. The third servant had merely hidden his talent in the ground and was punished by his master.

For Calum, Jesus added a fourth servant. The fourth servant invested his talents and lost them all on a venture that did not pay off. When the master returned, what do you think he said to that servant who held out empty hands?

The result from this servant was worse than from the servant who had buried his one talent and returned it to the master."

John Malcolm sat back and closed his single eye in thought.

"The effort was good, but the result was bad.

Sarai, this fourth servant was never mentioned in church and he was not in the Bible either."

"That is true," said Sarai, "but you know the answer because you know the Lord.

The master commended this servant, because, although he had failed, he had taken a risk and been faithful. This is a thing that the Lord loves. Faithfulness and success are not the same thing, and the Lord loves faithfulness more than He loves success.

John Malcolm, the Lord wants you to have this story for two reasons.

First, you lost your eye while working hard and honestly. That is why your eye was not healed when you first arrived in heaven. Your missing eye is a badge of honor. Keep it a while longer.

Second, you and Emilie chose to beget three children. Children are a risk at the best of times. You lost one son to alcohol. You lost your daughter to Colitis. Begetting and raising your three children was done with faithfulness and risk, but not complete success. For this the Master honors you."

Sarai rose and went to the stove. She retrieved the black carpet from yesterday's telling of the Black Death and brought it to John.

"Close your eye, John Malcolm," Sarai commanded, "I will show you a truth."

As John closed his eye, Sarai flipped the black carpet over to reveal a golden under side.

"Now open your eye, John Malcolm!

Look at the other side of the Black Death. It is pure gold. It is gold because there was so much faithfulness forgotten and unknown. A mother and father cared for children who died horribly and then perished themselves. A nun worked among the dying poor and succumbed later herself, her body unburied, her deeds un-remembered.

Oh, the lack of success, when fifty million died! The absence of results. The total loss, at least to the human eye.

We measured success. The Maker measured faithfulness. Touch this lively golden weave under the ashes of death.

Thank you, John Malcolm, for the times when you failed, but were faithful to the Lord."

John reached his right hand up to the empty socket, where the eye had been.

"I always wore sunglasses or turned my face away from

the camera. The empty place, roughly sewn together, where an eye should have been, was ugly."

Sarai reached across and put her hand on John Malcolm's, just where the eye had been.

"Today I pray the Creator's blessing on this scar. On our last day in this tent, I will tell you where to find healing. But even after you receive a living eye, a scar will remain, like the badge of honor on a soldier's uniform, to remind you.

Wear that scar with pride and thanks.

Well done, good and faithful servant."

CALUM

BATTLES WON AND LOST

When John Malcolm returned the next day, he pulled a black eye patch from his pocket and handed it to Sarai.

"I used this for many a year, ashamed of my missing eye. Now the scar is a badge of honor and I will wear it openly."

Sarai placed the eye patch on her stovetop and smiled.

"In this tent, I have seen all manner of wounds. Many, like your eye, were misunderstood and poorly worn on the other side.

Today I will tell you about a soldier, Lars Bengtson. He came to this tent about two hundred years ago, with wounds far worse than yours, and all unseen. It took him longer than you to understand his wounds. Not all of them were marks of honor, but some were. The Creator wants you to have his story, but I am not sure why. Perhaps after the telling, we will know."

John seated himself in his place and Sarai started the story while preparing two cups of tea.

"In the year 1700, 10,000 Swedish soldiers defeated a Russian force four times as large. In that day, the Swedish Army was among the best in the world. Lars, without concern for his life, fought bravely, distinguished himself and brought honor to his regiment. After the battle, he was promoted to Captain of the Infantry.

Lars continued to lead well and matured as an officer. News of his feats and soldierly courage reached his village. When Lars went home on leave, his parents were proud of him. Neighbors brought gifts of food. Young women vied for his attention. Little boys playfully saluted him. Lars was a minor sensation in his small town, a soldier who had done well in service to God and country.

After a short and happy visit home in 1707, Lars returned to the army at its campaign base in Poland. There, the Swedish warrior King, Charles XII, was preparing for an assault on Russia. Lars found his regiment, and on August 22, 1707, Lars and 44,000 other Swedish soldiers began their march eastward.

Perhaps you read about The Great Northern War in your school days."

John placed his cup on the saucer and nodded.

"That was the end of Sweden's time as a great power. After that war, we became a normal country. Was Lars one of my ancestors?"

Sarai shook her head, no.

"Lars never had children, and you will see why in a moment. But you are descended from his younger brother.

Lars might have had children if Sweden had won the Battle of Poltava. I am sure you know that Sweden lost that battle and never recovered its former glory. I will not bore you with the details of the fight but just tell you about Lars.

Lars fought bravely, saw many of his regimental brothers killed gruesomely and, with the survivors, went into Russian captivity. His lot was not uncommon. Most of the Swedish soldiers that survived the battle were sent to Siberia.

During his career as a soldier, Lars saw things that a human should not see. It wounded him on the inside. On the way to Poltava he saw burned out villages, unburied dead and crow-eaten corpses. At the battle of Poltava, as in battles before that one, he saw his brothers torn by cannister fire, heard their suffering cries and held their hands as they died. In captivity, he did hard labor with little sympathy, far from home. Worst of all, the Great Northern War did not end until 1721, so his sojourn in Siberia lasted twelve long years.

Even in Tobolsk, Siberia, where his captive regiment was quartered, Lars' comrades noticed that he was not well. He kept to himself, read his Bible constantly, refused conversation and smiled seldom. He lost weight and lacked spirit. Modern armies called his condition "Shell Shock" and "PTSD." In Lars' time, they just said, 'he is not well.'

When the Treaty of Nystad ended the Great Northern War in 1721, Swedish captives had the right to return home. Lars joined the slow march westward, catching carts when he could, walking when none was available. Months later he arrived exhausted in his small village.

He stumbled into his village like a bedraggled scarecrow, wearing not the proud blue and gold uniform of a Swedish officer, but poorly fitting clothes donated by kindly civilians along the way. Little boys who would have saluted before, stood back in embarrassment; girls averted their eyes. His parents took him into the house. His mother drew the curtains.

The villagers' discomfort was nothing to Lars' own. He no longer belonged, and would never fit in. His mind was torn like a battlefield, with shell holes, acrid smoke and smells of death. Lars had seen things no human should see. He was no longer useful to polite society."

"I knew men like that from the First World War," said John. "I worked with veterans on construction jobs. Most were fine, but a few were of no use. They could not hold a job or stay in a family. Some drank themselves to death."

"Lars did not drink, but everything else you said was true

of him. He lived near the church in an abandoned carriage shed. He survived on hand-outs. Lars was not unkind to villagers, but he did not join in village life. He stood aside, seemed to live in his own world. He talked to himself and read his Bible, sometimes aloud in the hearing of villagers. He did not contribute to the welfare of the village."

"It is hard to see the Creator praising him," said John. "What use was he? In America, we called people like Lars, 'Street People.'"

"When Lars was in this tent," replied Sarai, "I showed him different carpets than I have shown you. The Creator's healing was strange. I showed Lars carpet after carpet of successful men. Rich men. Powerful ones. Famous. Proud. Names you would know.

I pulled out the carpet of Alexander the Great. Seldom do I use that one! Alexander's conquests were unprecedented, and all by the time he was thirty. And the story of Peter the Great of Russia, who had defeated the Swedes at Poltava. He was a bold and successful leader, who turned Russia into a great power. Finally, I showed him the carpet of a nobleman near Lars' village. The Count lived in a castle with his many children. His walls were covered with art and his barns were full of well-bred horses. He never went outside without silk stockings and tailored suits.

When Lars came back after many days of these stories, I asked him if the pain was less, the wounds healed.

He sat where you are sitting and smiled at me. He told me something strange which I have never forgotten."

"I was not successful," he said. "I owned nothing. Lived on hand-outs. Bore no children. Left no inheritance. Powerless. Uncomfortable. Restless. Homeless. The opposite of all your stories.

I was sent as a sign.

When a villager hurried past me, chasing a vain thing, I was a sign.

I was a sign to the young men going to the army.

When the Count came to church with his beautiful family, I stood like a scarecrow with a Bible in my hand.

A sign."

John frowned at the thought.

"I don't understand his usefulness. Would it not have been better if he had learned a trade and provided for himself?"

"I had the same thought," replied Sarai. "But years later, I met his younger brother. When Lars died in 1748 at the age of 71, the entire village gathered to bury him. By then his parents were gone. He had no grieving widow or children. The Parson seemed at a loss for words as they lowered Lars into the ground.

An old man near the front of the crowd started a hymn and the others joined in. It seemed right to honor Lars with thanks to God for his solitary life, lived at the edge of the village.

The Parson found his voice after the hymn.

'Lars was not like us. We all noticed that. He made us think about things. He had nothing. Just his Bible and God. And a little spare kindness from us.

Maybe that was enough."

That was the shortest sermon the Parson ever preached. It was a eulogy that Lars' would have approved.

Then the old wife of the man who had led the hymn, said what the rest of the villagers were thinking.

'Lars was a sign.

Pointing us to the skies.'

After that, they buried him with more tears than an unrelated stranger deserved."

Sarai finished thoughtfully and sat still.

"Why do you think the Lord wanted you to have Lars' story?"

"Because," said John, "I was given many signs. But I

might as well have been blind in both eyes for missing so many of them."

"Signs are easy to miss," said Sarai.

"The church in Simlangsdalen had a steeple that pointed to the skies. But it became common, just a piece of architecture. A sign must be something unusual that catches our attention, like a ragged man in a carriage shed.

Often a sign is unpleasant and unwanted.

The most common sign in the world is the Cross, a symbol of execution. Jesus asked, if it were possible, for that cup to pass from him.

If a daughter stops talking to you. That is one kind of sign.

If a daughter goes astray. That is another sign.

If a daughter's life is shortened, that is the hardest of all, and far beyond any sign.

Like every death, your daughter's death reminded that life's little day was ebbing swiftly out,

And pointed to the skies."

LARS

THE YEAR 1918

When John Malcolm returned to Sarai's tent the next day, he expressed growing anticipation to see his daughter and others who had preceded him.

Sarai thanked John for the threads he had added to her carpets. His stories would comfort and lighten the path for others to follow.

"You are almost ready to go forward," she said.

"Up to now," she told John, "I showed you carpets from your family's past. Each story was a weave from your genealogy. Going backward is one way to understand suffering. I hope that these stories have been useful."

"They are beautiful stories and helped me understand many things," said John.

"Going backward helps people understand life on the other shore. Going beyond one's own life and family is also necessary. On the other side, we did not see life in neighborhoods other than our own.

Today and tomorrow I am going to tell you stories from outside your family, from other communities."

Sarai placed two carpets on the floor near John's feet.

"For my two stories, I have chosen the year 1918.

What were you doing in the year 1918, John Malcolm?"

"I was in America, married to Emilie. I worked as a plasterer and we had managed to purchase our first small house. Not bad for having emigrated just six years earlier!

Our first child Reynold was born in 1920. Emilie was pregnant in 1919. In 1918, we were building our lives in the new world."

"Yes, you were busy. Did you consider yourself happy?"

"Oh yes! Other than losing an eye, I had done very well. Emilie and I were healthy and active. We lived among other immigrants all striving to succeed. At home we spoke Swedish and we traded letters with our relatives back home. In comparison to life on the farm in Sweden, our lives were exciting and rich."

"What about the Great War?" asked Sarai. "Or the Spanish Flu of 1918?"

"We heard about those things and knew people who were affected, but these events did not touch us."

"And you were fortunate they did not. The Great War devastated an entire continent, destroying a generation of young men. Thirty million were killed, wounded or missing.

The Spanish flu killed fifty million worldwide, including strong young men like you.

You missed some tragedies in peaceful little Minneapolis.

We will not speak of millions of Chinese, Indians and Africans in 1918. Their lives were hard and often short.

In the year 1918, Russian Bolsheviks killed the last Tsar and his family and dumped their bodies down a mine shaft. Just another footnote from that year."

"Yes," said John, "We were extremely fortunate compared to all of those people. We did not understand that at the time. They lived far away. Now I understand that the year 1918 was a lot harder for others than it was for us."

Sarai pointed to one of the two carpets at John's feet, a beautiful carpet in reds, greens and whites. In the center was a castle and around the edges, various coats of arms.

To understand how blessed you were in 1918, I will show you two carpets. They are both from the land of Hungary, not nearly as far away from Minnesota as China. And yet, the year 1918 in Hungary could not have been more different than 1918 in Minneapolis or even Sweden.

This carpet tells the story of a Count. His path crossed that of a woman born the same year as you, in 1887. She was from a village named Polgar, and in 1918 she was a Communist.

The carpets of the Count and the Communist will take us beyond your family, into the wider world. For some reason, the Maker wants you to have these two stories."

THE COUNT

My first story is about a Count named Gyula Andrassy, who was born in 1860. His father built a beautiful castle in a little town called Tiszadob. The castle had four entrances, one for each season; twelve towers for the months of the year; 52 rooms for the weeks of the year and 365 windows for the days.

The castle was a fairy tale, full of stained glass, fine carpets, ornately carved furniture, huge paintings and Venetian mirrors. The gardens were spectacular and the surrounding forests full of game. Gyula was 25 years old when the castle was completed. He spent many happy days in its halls; hunted for game in the surrounding woods and fished in nearby lakes.

Neither little Tiszadob nor the region around it had anything as spectacular as that castle.

As the Count grew older, he became a great leader, the Foreign Minister of Austria-Hungary. He was a patriot who wanted the best for his country when Europe was falling apart.

You mentioned yesterday that you knew veterans form the Great War. You heard about the horrors done on the battlefields of Europe."

"Yes," said John, "We all heard about the Great War. I immigrated to America in 1912, just before the war started. The American Army did not require me to join as I was already 24 years old. Many younger men went to fight. After the war, most came home to a warm welcome. A few perished and some returned with shell shock."

Sarai continued, "Gyula, as Foreign Minister of Hungary, worked hard to avoid that war. He led a peace team to try to find solutions. He failed. The war came.

When, after years of bloodshed, he saw that Austria-Hungary would lose, he tried to negotiate peace. Again, he failed.

He worked long days before and during the war. As the war wound down, he redoubled his efforts. He wrote letters. Made phone calls. Received visitors. Gave speeches. Convinced delegations. Chaired meetings.

Count Gyula did what he could.

Whenever public duties exhausted him and he found a little time, he took a train north to Tiszadob. A driver met his family at the train station and brought them to their beloved castle. There Gyula and his family rested; awoke to fine breakfasts, hot coffee and beautiful views. Gyula hunted and fished, re-gained his energy for bureaucratic battles in Vienna and intrigues in Budapest.

In 1918, the year of your happiness in Minneapolis, the Great War ended with disaster for Hungary. Thousands of young men had perished. Those who returned from the front felt betrayed and angry. The country they returned to was poor. They had no future. Tempers frayed.

At a large gathering in Budapest, speakers climbed on shoulders and harangued the soldiers to overthrow the monarchy. There were so many ideas in the air that no one could later remember which ones took hold. Word spread across the country that people should rise-up and demand justice. Everyone was talking at the same time. The loudest voices were the angriest ones.

A confused revolution spread across the country. Far to the north in a town called Polgar, a woman born the same year as you, climbed on the hood of a truck and gave an impassioned speech. She convinced fifty angry townspeople to join her on a night ride north, to Tiszadob.

They planned to attack the castle.

TISZADOB CASTLE

THE COMMUNIST

Anna Horvath was born poor. A poor Hungarian woman who wanted to improve her lot, had two options. She could marry up or she could emigrate to the new world. Anna had not married up. Janos' family was just as poor as hers. When the Army called him to fight the Italians and other enemies of Hungary, Anna and their ten-year-old son, Lajos, saw him off at the train station. That was the last time she and Lajos saw him. He was killed fighting in Italy in 1915.

When the war ended in 1918, Anna was a 32-year-old widow with a teenage son and no prospects. At war's end, waiting women snatched up the few returning soldiers.

Anna's anger had been growing since 1915 when news of her husband's death reached the village of Polgar. The State's small death payment was soon gone. She lived in a rented house at the edge of town in exchange for her labor and that of her son. In a few years, Lajos would decide whether to move to the big city as a laborer or stay in Polgar as a farm hand.

When rabble rousers appeared in Polgar to preach revolution and the end of injustice, Anna was fertile ground. No one had to convince her that something was deeply wrong with the world. She had nothing at all to lose and joined the movement.

Her anger quickly gained the attention of the other revolutionaries and they often listened to her. Her voice was a spark in Polgar's dry tinder.

On a cool night in November, Anna's call to raid the castle in Tiszadob, was answered by fifty of her townmates. They commandeered eleven cars and trucks and headed north. With burning torches and rifles in hand, they leapt from the vehicles into the castle courtyard. Six castle caretakers fled in terror. Anna and her rabble owned the night.

The revolutionaries loaded furniture and valuables onto the trucks. They broke 365 windows, smashed mirrors and slashed the canvass of paintings. Using sledge-hammers and picks, the Polgarians reduced to kindling any furniture too large to carry.

On the way back to Polgar, the hollering and whooping crowd downed bottles of fine wine raided from the castle's cellar. They had righted a wrong and it was glorious. The damnable Count responsible for death, poverty and destruction had been punished.

Back in Polgar, Anna dragged a large chair from the back of a truck into her rented room and slept soundly for the first time in weeks."

Sarai interrupted her story with a tired sigh, "John Malcolm, this kind of story is as old as our race. My carpets are full of them. There were haves and have nots. They fought over things. From here, both sides look foolish. But over there, the fighting was ceaseless, and everyone had elaborate stories to explain their feelings and actions.

They were just things, John Malcolm.

How did it go with your possessions?"

John touched his chin thoughtfully, "I built a house on a lake and Emilie filled it with furniture, Swedish clothing, ceramics, paintings. It was not a castle, but it contained the remnants of our lives. The old photos meant a lot to us."

"That is how it was with the Count," said Sarai.

"The castle meant something to him. When he heard that it had been ransacked, he never returned to Tiszadob. Ten years later, in 1929, he died far away.

Anna never became rich and her revolution fell apart. Later, when Anna was sixty-years-old, Communists took over Hungary, with the help of Soviet troops. By then, no one pretended that Communism had anything to do with justice.

One day Anna was at home when old Mrs. Szabo dropped by with some fresh jam. Anna motioned for Mrs. Szabo to have a seat and cleared her a spot on the castle chair.

Mrs. Szabo laughed and dropped herself into the chair.

'You should be happy, Anna. You have the Count's chair. I am a Countess for sitting in it.'

Anna reached out to feel the carved arm of the wooden chair. It was a very nice chair, nicer than anything else in her house.

'Yes,' said Anna, 'it is a good chair. I remember the night I took it.

Four years ago, in 1944, everyone was taking furniture again, this time from the Jews. I did not take any. I already had a chair.

The chair did not bring me happiness and the furniture from the Jews will not bring happiness either.

Thank you for the jam.'

After Mrs. Szabo left, Anna sat quietly with the jam jar in her lap. Her anger had softened over the years, because of age and the birth of a grandson.

She would have returned the chair if she could have, but the Count had died, and the castle was an orphanage."

Sarai pushed Anna's carpet nearer to that of the Count's. There was a chair woven into Anna's carpet with the words, "Butorok a tied," meaning "the furniture is yours."

Sarai put her hand on the woven chair.

"When Anna was here, she told me she regretted that night. She wished she could have made it right. She looked forward to meeting the Count at the Forum, as equals, to tell him how sorry she was.

Of course, neither of them will care about the chair when they meet. The evil deed itself will have been paid for many years ago, before the chair was taken.

The Count would also say he was sorry. He did not use his lavish possessions in the past life to succor poor people, like Anna.

John Malcolm, the failure, the loss, the sadness we suffered, were as nothing to the wrongs that we did to one another.

The Maker suffered with us. More mysterious, the Maker stayed his hand as we hurt each other.

The wrongs we did, John Malcolm, were many and great. Now we realize how terrible.

Sometimes, on the other side, we also knew it.

When we knew it, like Anna, even if we had wanted to return the furniture, we could not.

They were all dead,

some taken by old age,

others by rail cars.

That was not the Creator's world.

That was ours.

John Malcolm, the Creator wanted you to have these stories. At the Forum there will be those who ask your forgiveness and others from whom you will beg pardon. Each account has been settled, every wrong righted. But there is work you must do.

You will not be alone in this work. Deep magic was done on a table of sacrifice. The Creator did not look away as some thought. The Creator never looked away. He looked hard at it, without blinking, and took the matter on Himself.

Because,
we could not return the furniture.

I have finished my second story."

John rose from his seat and paced the floor in front of Sarai's stove.

"I have much to ask pardon for."

"You are ready to go forward," said Sarai. "There are many who want to meet you. Some you loved. Some you wronged. Some you did not know.

There will be no shadows.

The old has passed away.

Tomorrow I will tell you my last story."

ANNA

FELLOWSHIP OF SUFFERING

When John arrived at Sarai's tent for her last story, it was clear that she had been busy. Two colorful carpets draped the front of her tent and bamboo poles propped the tent flap open.

She greeted John with a smile and invited him to sit inside while she finished folding a carpet. John ducked into the tent, removed his shoes and poured two cups of tea.

Sarai entered a few minutes later and sat next to the stove. She took her first sip of tea and laughed.

"This tea is not bad, John Malcolm. You have learned much in your weeks here!"

John winked with his good eye and reminded Sarai that he had merely poured tea that had already been prepared and steeped.

"That is true," said Sarai, "and that is what I want to show you today. You poured what had already been prepared. Someone else planted the tea bush, another tended it over years, yet others harvested the leaves. Time would fail me to tell who dried the leaves, shipped them to us, infused this tea with rose hips. What wondrous labor by so many brought this tea to our lips!

We have not even spoken of he who mined white clay for

this porcelain, she who turned the cup at wheel, they who painted, baked and fired this Fine China. We give thanks to the Creator for each of them.

Later I shall wash the cups and saucers.

Now, in the middle, we drink. It is no small thing to drink. Without our drinking, the work of those before and after would be in vain. The Creator is pleased also with us, our smelling, tasting and each swallow."

John swirled the tea in his cup appreciatively and set the cup and saucer on the small table to his right.

"I never thought about all that," he said. "We are in the middle of a stream. This knowledge makes the tea sweeter."

Sarai laid a carpet over John's knees and returned to her place by the stove.

"You learned that your missing eye is a badge of honor. Even when your eye is healed, a small scar will remain to remind you that God loves your faithfulness.

Today I will tell you about your other scar."

John was confused. "My other scar? I have some small scratches and marks, but no other scar."

"You do have another scar and it is a most important one. Reach your hand down and feel at the center of your stomach. You never thought of this small indentation as a scar. You barely thought of it at all. In Sweden, you called it a 'navel' and your American children called it a 'belly button.' Few took this scar seriously on the other side,

but your mother did.

Your mother was in this tent and told me her story. Some of it you know. Some that you know, you never thought about. Today we will think on those things.

When your mother sat where you are now, she told me of your birth, and I wove it into this carpet. Put your finger there on that woven bed. The figure at its foot is a midwife. There is your father, waiting in another room.

Your father could hear your mother's cries, but births in

Sweden were not for men to see. Your mother's contractions became more frequent. The pain increased. The midwife wiped your mother's brow with cool water and held her hand. Your mother pushed. The top of your head appeared, with dark hair. Then your face, eyes shut tightly. Shoulders, chest, tiny stomach.

Ah, there,

the cord!

The cord through which your mother had fed you!

And then,

aha,

you were a boy child.

The midwife held you. She laid you on your mother's stomach, cord still attached for a minute more.

You cried.

Your mother wept with pleasure.

The thing was done.

The midwife cut the cord and tied a tiny knot next to your belly. She covered your mother with a blanket, washed her hands and invited your father into the room.

There. There he is, bending over you and your mother, kissing her cheek."

John Malcolm tenderly caressed the carpet's threads. Tears ran freely from his good eye.

"Well you may cry, John Malcolm. Well you may cry. It is a powerful thing.

There was pleasure in your making. There was goodness. Well-loved food. Drink. Laughter. Anticipation and Joy.

And there was pain.

Suffering. In every birth there was suffering. Since the beginning.

If you could trace each cord from belly to mother, from belly to mother, from belly to mother, it would reach back to the beginning of our race, like a chain of love, a fellowship of suffering. To be in this stream is to be connected to each one that begat another, and another, and begat you, and beyond you will beget yet more.

No one sought suffering on the other side. It was a holy thing to relieve suffering. The Savior healed when He walked the earth. Took away pain.

And yet, there was also about suffering a sacred wonder. Sometimes it was a privilege to be among the fellowship of suffering.

You already know about the cross, the dying there. When the crowd looked up, they saw the hands nailed to the wood, the bloody visage from the thorns.

If they had looked closely, they would also have seen a navel. Perhaps only one person standing among the many saw the navel.

She wept for her son. She remembered the night thirty-three years before, the pain, the contractions, the cord.

That also is the story of Christmas, John Malcolm.

The noble suffering of Mary.

And later, so many more suffered and considered it a privilege. A cloud of witnesses:

They were tortured. Had trial of cruel mockings and scourgings.

Of bonds and imprisonment.

They were stoned. They were sawn asunder.

Tempted, slain with the sword.

They wandered about in sheepskins and goatskins.

Destitute, afflicted, tormented.

Of whom the world was not worthy.

These also are our mothers and fathers. We are among them in the fellowship of suffering.

Sometimes your suffering, John Malcolm, was a sacred thing."

John and Sarai sat quietly for a long time.

Finally, John broke the silence.

"How can I thank you for your stories, Sarai?"

Sarai rose from her seat and led John through the opening at the front of her tent. She pointed to two carpets draped on the front.

"You can take these two forward for me. They are complete and will comfort some who sat in my tent long ago. One will go to a woodworker in the forest of Gilead. The other you will bring to the Forum where you will meet your Gloria, your Emilie and your dear mother and father.

There, for the first time, you will know how to rightly thank your parents. There you will love Gloria and Emilie as you never could before.

You will see, John Malcolm, if you have not seen already, that in heaven the best is always and forever, yet to be."

John took the two carpets and hoisted them onto his shoulder. He asked Sarai if he might return in the future for more stories.

Sarai laughed.

"Oh yes John Malcolm! You are always welcome here. There are so many more stories to tell.

And you make the most delicious tea!"

A BALM IN GILEAD

John Malcolm rose early and loaded Sarai's two carpets onto the back of his camel. The camel and John walked toward the eastern edge of the oasis. Meddur, the Nigerian from the oasis' café, accompanied John for several miles and then gave him final instructions for the onward journey.

Before returning to the oasis, Meddur pressed a package into John's hands.

"This is from Sarai. She said to open it after your eye is healed," he said. "She and the rest of us in Al Amin, wish you God's mercy as you travel onward. Come back and visit us any time."

John thanked Meddur and watched him return to the dark shadow of desert palms that marked the oasis.

John and his solitary camel plodded forward, step after trackless step through the dry place.

After many days and nights, small changes appeared. A bony shrub here, dry grass in a ravine, a cloud the size of a man's hand in the east.

Gradually, John and his camel knew that they were in the Sahel, a transition between desert and forest. Finally, the first trees appeared, at first small and then larger, and finally as big as houses. To love a tree truly, one must live where they are few.

Yaw, a forest Woodsmith from Ghana, was gathering wood when he encountered John Malcolm and his camel from the desert. Yaw welcomed them and suggested that the camel could be thanked, unburdened and returned, riderless, to the desert. Yaw invited John for an early lunch, hoisted a beam-sized branch on his shoulder and led him to a large tree encircled by a winding staircase.

The staircase climbed round the tree upward, ingeniously supported by branches, or by hemp cables slung from higher limbs. When they reached a shaded patio, John and Yaw peered from the high branches to see a huge tree, thousands of years old at the center. Yaw told John that this was the Tree of Life bearing healing produce. Balms, lotions and elixirs from its fruit were exported across the land. The extravagantly carved structure intertwined with the Tree of Life was a cathedral for worship and a clinic for the injured.

"I suspect, by looking at your missing eye," said Yaw, "that you are headed for the Tree of Life and the clinic there. We call this place Gilead. It is a place of healing."

"Yes," replied John, "The Lord directed me here.

After I am healed, I will go forward to meet my daughter, wife and parents. There will also be many others at a place called the Forum."

"Tomorrow," said Yaw, "I will take you to the clinic in the Tree of Life and introduce you to Dr. Samuel Harvey. He will make a diagnosis and prescribe treatment. No one leaves here un-healed, though it takes years for some."

"Years?" asked John surprised. "I am anxious to go forward to meet my loved-ones. All I need is an eye!"

"Dr. Harvey will explain further," replied Yaw, "but your loved ones will enjoy you more after your treatment is complete. You will also like yourself better."

John went to sleep puzzled by Yaw's words and awoke the next day eager to start his treatment.

Yaw accompanied John to the clinic high in the Tree of Life and introduced him to the receptionist, Samantha. Samantha smiled at John and directed him to a couch and the reading material on the table next to him. John thumbed a copy of 'The Lorax' and a short biography of Gollum from the Lord of the Rings, titled, "How I lost My Precious and Regained My Life."

When Dr Harvey arrived, he was not wearing a white Doctor's uniform, nor the blue scrubs of a lab technician. His clothing, what there was of it, was wildly colorful, and behind his bushy beard was a mischievous smile.

Dr Harvey invited John into his office and asked him the purpose of his visit.

"Well," said John Malcolm, "You can see that I have a missing eye. Since this is heaven, I was hoping you could fix that, especially before I see my wife and daughter. My daughter never saw me with two eyes. It would be a nice surprise."

Doctor Harvey threw his head back with laughter.

"John, your eye is the easy part! There is so much more. Some of it you do not even know about.

The Lord sent you here to be thoroughly changed.

John, you cannot leave yourself, take a vacation from yourself. You must change yourself. I am here to help you do that.

There are those who choose to stay on the other side. They do not want to change, and the Lord does not force them. That you are here on this side is a mercy, but it will not be easy. Your healing will be more like hard physical therapy than a simple pill."

John squinted at Doctor Harvey with his good eye. He was not sure the Doctor was being serious, since Harvey could not stop smiling and there were deep laugh lines at the corners of his eyes.

"Let me explain," said Harvey, "you have an inner blindness more serious than your missing eye. You were only half alive on the other side. You wanted things that were wrong and empty. You developed bad habits - I will call them grooves – that must be stripped away by hard work. You have forgotten how to be free, how to dance wildly, to let yourself be ecstatically happy.

Come here, John. Look out this window on the field below."

John walked to the window and looked down. He saw girls skipping and dancing with flowers woven into their hair. Boys playing tag with flour-filled stockings and splashing water. There was a ball game, a painting class, violin lessons. Maenids, faeries, unicorns, dogs and animals of every sort caroused with joy and abandon. John was not sure if the field was a circus, a festival, a school, or all three at the same time.

Harvey let the lesson sink in as John's eye followed the riotous activity.

"Those are my patients. Anything could happen down there, John, absolutely anything! You are watching what it is like to be healed.

To play like that is far beyond getting a new eye."

John stood transfixed. A memory, long forgotten, from deep childhood came to his mind.

He was the first in Flahult to own a bicycle. He had always been a fast runner, but after he mastered the art of bike-balance, he could fly like a swift deer. Once, as he careened down the dirt road toward town, he felt a surge of joy coursing through his body like lightning. He screamed at the top of his lungs, "Frihet!" - freedom! And screamed again, even raising both hands skyward in happiness.

He tasted, smelled and felt that moment of unbridled joy for the first time in almost ninety years.

John sat down thoughtfully.

"I would like to be like that again, at least some of the time."

Harvey pointed to a chart on the wall.

"Can you read that chart, John?"

John squinted his eye and read the word "GROOVES."

"As you grew older, you developed grooves, John. The grooves are holding you back. I will help you get rid of them.

Look under the title and read to me the first groove.

John squinted again and read,

"Arguing like an old married couple."

"Oh dear," said John, "how did you know about that?"

Harvey laughed again, "John, are you my first patient?

You developed a way of dealing with Emilie and she with you. She said a little thing, mumbled in Swedish. That would set you off. You called her 'crazy' and rolled your eye. That was a groove.

You did it many times. You must lose it here.

When you see Emilie again, it will be fresher than when you walked her home on the last night of English class. And neither of you will ever develop bad grooves again!"

"Read the next groove," said Harvey.

"What can you do for me?" read John.

Harvey asked John to hold out his hands and felt the rough callouses.

"You were a plasterer, so this was not as bad for you as for diplomats, Hollywood producers, politicians and businesspeople. People developed the groove of evaluating every person they met based on their usefulness. He is a customer. She a voter. An important contact. A beautiful woman. Ambassador. General. Mr. President.

Do we care about any of that here?

You must be joking!

The Rabbi, Jesus (he was Jewish, by the way), showed a better way. He spent time with people who were of no use to him. He did not care what clothes they wore, what title they possessed or what make of donkey they drove. He liked them a lot more if their net worth was less and their house was smaller.

He did not drop names.

Upside down.

He was a revolutionary.

They killed him.

You saw a woman on the bus.

What was your groove?

It was such a waste that even you tired of it sometimes. You evaluated her, not openly like an Italian or an Arab, but more like a sneaky Swede. Too old. Too young. Too big. Too small. Just right.

Enough already! They are all just right. Every single one a child of God, is worth your time.

Stop it with the sneaky Swede approach to grooves. Up here we are going to be open and talk about things.

Read the next groove, John Malcolm.

John again squinted and read,

"Bitterness."

"And the next, John," said Harvey.

"Self-defense."

"Next!" cried Harvey.

"Excuses."

Harvey rose from his chair and grasped John by the shoulders, shaking him vigorously.

"Do we have work to do, John Malcolm?

Do you want to be free and fully alive again? Regain the best of your youth?

If I let you go to the rendezvous like this, what would they say? Would they be happy that I let into a perfect gathering of roses, a smelly weed?

You would spoil everything. Gloria and Emilie are

expecting you to be healed before they meet you. Just as they have been healed.

John Malcolm and Doctor Harvey sat in silence for a moment.

Finally, Doctor Harvey dabbed his fingers into a light brown balm and touched John's missing eye.

He closed his eyes and repeated soft words in Hebrew.

"This begins the healing of your eye, John Malcolm, and the healing of so much more."

John felt a tingling where his eye had been. He smiled. It was beginning.

"Tomorrow we will meet again," said Dr. Harvey.

"We will continue our treatment.

You can play on that field any time you want.

Samantha will make your next appointment and take your co-payment."

"My co-payment?" asked John.

Dr. Harvey threw his head back and roared with laughter.

"Well, I can try, can't I?"

SARAI'S PACKAGE

After many months in Gilead, John Malcolm was ready to resume his journey to the Rendezvous. Eye healed, grooves gone, years shed, John rose from his cot and prepared his pack for the walk east.

The day before, he had thanked Doctor Harvey and Samantha. Now it was time to eat a final breakfast with Yaw.

John sat at the patio table across from Yaw and placed Sarai's package between them.

"This package is from Sarai, the carpet weaver in Al Amin, who told my life through the ancestors' eyes. She told me to open this package after my eye was healed. If you don't mind, I would like to open it with you, before I leave."

Yaw paused from breaking bread and motioned for John to proceed.

John untied the ribbon and tore open the wrapping. Inside was a small box. John opened the box to reveal the black eye patch he had given Sarai earlier and a single sheet of paper.

John picked up the eye patch and handed it to Yaw.

"I wore this for many a year to cover the ugliness of my missing eye. In Sarai's tent I learned that my scar was a badge of honor. I promised Sarai, after her story about

Calum, the Scottish sea captain, that I would never hide my ugliness again and gave her this patch as a pledge."

"Now," said Yaw, "she has returned it to you. What does her note say?"

John unfolded the sheet of paper and found in careful lettering, the following message from Sarai:

Dear John Malcolm:

Now that your eye is healed and you have been thoroughly changed, I want to tell you two things that you would not have understood before.

First, much of your disappointment on the other shore was your own fault. Dr. Harvey is famous for his treatment of grooves. With your grooves gone, you understand how they caused you and everyone around you, needless pain and useless suffering. Congratulations on your healing.

Second, now that your eyesight is fully restored, I will tell you the parable of the four-paned window above the main entrance of Tiszadob's castle.

The top left pane was the clearest. That pane represented what you knew about yourself and what others knew about you. A lot of what you and they thought about you was wrong. But that was then. This pane has been washed clean.

The top right glass was what you knew about yourself, but others did not know. These were the things you hid from others because of shame. Dr. Harvey called this pane your sneaky Swedish side. It was opaque but is now clear. You are without shame as before the rebellion.

The lower left window was what others knew about you, but you did know not about yourself. They were too polite to tell you, or thought you too stubborn to bear the truth. Your pride prevented their knowledge from penetrating your thick skull. Dr. Harvey called this pane your stubborn Swedish side. This pane was dark but is now light, because you do not fear others or their honesty.

The lower right pane represents what you did not know about yourself, and others did not know about you either. On the other side, we did not understand ourselves well. We woke up happy, or sad, or had these thoughts or those deeds. We knew not why. We were a mystery to ourselves, and not a pleasant one. We saw through a glass darkly.

The Holy Spirit cleared this pane each night while you slept in Gilead.

John Malcolm, once you were blind, but now you see. Once you saw through a glass darkly but now you see as you are seen.

That is why I returned your patch to you. Wear it round your neck with honor. Proclaim through this wearing the feast of sight, the glory of full vision.

These colors you have by God's hand.
From brilliant lights and hues,
To subtle shades and shadows,
To see,
To clearly see!
And never be blind again!

Yours from the tent of telling,
Sarai

John folded the paper and placed it in his breast pocket.

Yaw removed a necklace from his own neck and tied the eye patch carefully where a pendant hung. Once the patch was secured, he leaned across the table and motioned for John to bow his head.

Yaw looped the necklace around John's neck and fastened the clip.

John raised his head and looked across the table at Yaw. For the first time in many decades, tears of happiness rolled down, both cheeks.

WASHING

After breakfast with Yaw, John Malcolm joined a dozen other travelers for a journey to the Forum. The Forum is a week by foot from Gilead and sits astride the road to the Great City, serving as a marketplace, a rest stop and, most importantly, a rendezvous. The carpets of Al Amin adorn its walls, floors and courtyards.

John and his companions walked eagerly on a marked path, downhill to the bottom of a valley. When the path reached level ground, they wound through forest and finally found themselves beside a pleasant stream.

A crowd of travelers was at the water's edge. A child, no more than twelve, faced them from mid-stream. He was waist deep in the water.

The crowd grew silent as the youth began to speak.

"You have come from Gilead. You will soon be at the Forum.

This stream is called "What might have been" and "If only."

Bring into this water your regrets. Lay in the wetness. Slip under the surface. Splash yourself. Drink.

Once a man named Jacob came here with his favorite son Joseph. On the other side, Joseph's brothers had sold him into slavery because of their jealousy. The brothers had lived to regret their deed and repented of it when Joseph was made ruler of all Egypt.

Jacob and Joseph had thought themselves blameless victims.

But in Gilead, they were healed and their eyes were opened.

With open eyes, Jacob thought, 'if only I had not played favorites amongst my wives and sons.'

And Joseph, seeing clearly, said, 'if only I had not been a spoiled braggart, and goaded my brothers to anger.'

With full seeing, their regrets grew in both size and number. They needed the washing of this stream.

On the other side, some said, 'I did my best, I did the best I could'

But now, we know the truth.

None of us did our best. We could all have done better. With your healing and your full sight, your regrets have grown.

Here, the Maker takes them upon Himself. After you cross this stream, your regrets will lose their bitter taste.

Welcome to the washing."

At this the boy, motioned them forward.

The crowd, his companions and John, entered the water. At first their feet wettened, then their knees. Up to their wastes, and higher.

The water began to work inward, a cleansing stream.

What she rued, fell away. What he neglected, slipped downriver.

John cupped his hands and poured saving liquid over his head. A better father, more perfect husband, the words spoken in anger, a kind word left unsaid. More water. More.

Oh, the regrets, so many and so deep!

It took a mighty washing in this river. A splashing and a ducking, a falling back into the water, arms cartwheeling.

Down, down, down into the water, the stains, troubles, regrets.

Finally, John Malcolm rose from the washing, rivulets of water running down his face and chest.

Waist deep in the stream he paused in silence. All the others quieted as one.

Sun overhead warmed their faces.

The child, the one who had invited them into the river, spoke a blessing.

"You are God's beloved children. He is well pleased with you."

John Malcolm waded through the water to the other side, lighter, younger, more ready than ever,

to meet his loved ones at the rendezvous.

They would speak of everything, remember picnics, walks, hands held, cheeks kissed. Laugh and cry, hold one another.

Even regrets, those could be remembered too. "I wish I had told you..."

But now, these had lost their weight. All their force was gone.

At the river, there had been a washing.

RENDEZVOUS

The Forum helps complete the work of Sarai. It is here that a traveler finds a lost friend or relative, or even a person never met before, but known through Sarai to be a key to their arrival on the safe shore.

The Forum is a place where time stands still. Before, there were not enough hours for the people we loved. There were those met too briefly, who deserved weeks or months. Like everything in Heaven, the Forum has no price, no limit, no check out, no deadline, no end.

As John set out, his heart raced with anticipation to see his loved ones, especially his dear wife Emilie and their daughter, Gloria. Gloria had died at the untimely age of 22, just as she was flowering into young womanhood. On the other side, John had never recovered from Gloria's loss. When he finally crossed over at the age of 97, Gloria's remembered face was the last image he saw.

Sarai's carpets, her tales, the ancestral journey backward in time, cleared his mind. Doctor Harvey's healing repaired the fissures in his heart. Yet only seeing Gloria again, in the presence of Emilie, would fully restore his loss.

As the travelers walked along a worn track, dotted with pines on both sides, John remembered Gloria's last weeks.

"There was the tearful phone call from Gloria in San Diego, telling Emilie that the doctor advised her return to Minneapolis for bed rest. Gloria the governess, who watched two young children, would be the daughter again. Gloria the young woman, trying to attract the right sort of sailor, would move back into her old bedroom.

It was defeat, no disguising the fact.

We silently packed the car for our drive west. We drove across America, stopped for gas when we had to, for food when required and for sleep late each evening. Long silences were broken by words of worry. Once at a gas station in New Mexico, the attendant asked if we were Germans.

"No," I said, "We are Americans from Sweden and our two boys are fighting in the Army and the Navy."

The attendant apologized for asking and washed the windshield extra clean.

When we arrived at Gloria's doorstep, I rang the bell, and Gloria appeared.

She had declined noticeably, lost weight, color, vigor. She fell into our arms sobbing uncontrollably.

It was not our way. It was not anyone's way. There was nothing for it, but to pack the car, thank the Holmgren's for their employment and care, and drive east.

The drive back took longer, with Gloria and Emilie in the back seat, whispering and sleeping by turns. More rest stops, bathroom breaks. Gloria could not hold down food.

It was a trip from hell.

The following weeks in Minneapolis were, if possible, worse.

Finally, the day came. I will not speak of it. It is impossible. Unbearable. It is not happening. We will awake from this, as from a nightmare.

The service was set for 10:30 a.m. on Saturday at Gustavus Adolphus Lutheran Church.

Flower wreaths arrived from Edison High School, the

Thespian Club, the Y, various friends, a few of my clients, the clothing store where Emilie worked.

The boys did not know yet. They were overseas in the service and mail was slow. They would learn by letter, that their sister had passed away. They would read the handwritten note from mother over and over in their respective bunks. Hide their tears. Go for walks. There was nothing for it, nothing to be done. A young man can die in war. A young woman should not die. It did not fit a category. Could not be sorted. What would they later say – our sister died during World War Two?

The guests arrived.

The Olsons, Sperries, Petersons, Nortons.

Gloria's theatre teacher and some others from the school. Her girlfriends. The boys were all gone.

Mrs. Clark, the Gold Star Mother. She knew about loss. But not a daughter.

Some people said nice things. Some said inappropriate things. Some said nothing. They were the best.

There was music. Standing. Sitting. Words.

The man in a robe at the front said more words. Cursed words. Nothing made sense. I just wanted to wake up from the terrible dream.

It was over. The guests filed by and made sympathetic comments. I had my sunglasses on. They could not see that my eye was red with crying, drooped with exhaustion.

We went to our cars, turned the headlights on. Robert, one of my plasterers, drove Emilie and I north in the motorcade to Sunset Memorial Park where we had five plots.

The police escort, with flashing lights, entered the cemetery grounds, parked at the side of the road. An officer emerged and stood at attention as cars drove past him to Gloria's final resting place."

John remembers and continues toward the Forum, climbing higher, a steep canyon on the left and on the right, carved into the mountainside, the ever winding and climbing trail. Two ridges more, there stands a peak. From that peak John and his companions know, they will look down upon a valley and see the dim outlines of the Forum.

John's memories of Gloria's last weeks are lamentation. Human memory was a fleeting thing on the other side, but no memory is lost in heaven, not even this one. It is redeemed, seen through better eyes. But not lost.

Nor even dimmed.

Some thought God was jealous of our earthly loves, for wives and daughters, sons and brothers.

God was never jealous of John's love for Gloria, nor indifferent to John's grief at her loss.

As the friends reach the peak and look down upon the wide valley, the outlines of the Forum come into view.

The travelers descend into the valley, their lungs full of free mountain air, hearts bursting with anticipation. They walk forward, then trot and finally run like madmen as they draw near.

A crowd has gathered at the Forum's western edge. Hundreds of people, eyes searching, hands waving.

John is running full tilt at the front, both eyes searching frantically for his Gloria.

A blonde girl, in a blue chiffon dress, breaks free and runs toward him. They both feel the power of it, as though each is the other, feet pounding, distance closing, the cosmos in a fit of ecstasy.

Explodes this reunion,
like a mad thing from heaven,
God's sides aching with laughter,
tears running down, sobs of pleasure.
Eye has not seen, nor ear heard.

Nor have entered into the heart of man, the things which God has prepared for those who love Him.

As if she understands the right order of things, Emilie

joins the glad embrace with patient grace minutes later. The three now healed, are joined in heaven, where time is gently unfolding, and the best is ever yet to be.

This night, like every night after the joy of reunion, the party of the Lord begins. Where hands touch and feet dance, the feast springs into life. Wine flows from huge vats that in the morning were full of mere water. Those formerly cautious, dance madly; those once fearful carouse with riotous joy. Deliriously happy humans join a feast that lasts late into the night.

Around the fires, the tables, the pools and fountains, they play, sing and dance with abandon. Earth had never seen a party like this one. The Forum Lord's wild heart burns with pleasure.

As the dancing slows and the morning lights begin to twinkle, the revelers drop off one by one into happy sleep, between friends, side by side, on the soft grass of the Forum.

Three lay down together, Gloria in the middle, her parents on either side. John lays on his left side, looks at Gloria's profile, her soft breathing. Across her face, he sees Emilie smiling with equal wonder.

John tenderly sweeps wisps of hair back from Gloria's ear and traces the folds with his fingers, the tiny curls, intricately fashioned folds.

Wonder of the Creator.

Across he sees Emilie and reaches for her. Their hands touch and then grasp one another, holding firmly, right over Gloria's navel. They cry softly together with joy and gladness, remembering how this all began, so long ago.

WONDER

As John's eyes close in sleep, a voice says, "come, I will show you a mystery."

John sees a hand beckoning him and grasps it.

"Sarai said much to you. You listened well and understood your suffering and griefs.

Now I will tell you why I allowed those things. Some you will comprehend. Some is beyond your language.

We are above Minnesota now. Look under the Willow tree in your back yard on Pierce Street. There is a pleasant breeze. The sun is shining. Branches sway lazily and rhythmically. Your daughter is lying under the tree looking up at the sky through shimmering Willow leaves.

She is turning clouds into animals and telling herself a story.

Gloria and her imagination were wonderful. I like her and her visions."

John peers down and sees dreamy wonder on this daughter's face.

"Yes," he says, "I like her too."

He flies higher and he feels himself crossing fields of space and time.

"Look at Lars on the field of battle. He is loading his

musket while shot flies past him on every side. He is steady. This is before Sarai's story when he came home broken.

Lars and his self-sacrifice are amazing. Lars and his bravery gave me joy."

John looks at Lars, in his blue and gold uniform, running toward the enemy, heedless of his safety.

"I would like to meet Lars someday," he says.

Over a sparkling sea the voice whispers with love,

"Calum!

He took such a chance on his idea. Watch the Lady Fife's prow cut through the blue sea as Calum and his ship sail south to Cornwall.

Calum and his lust for new things are treasures I hold dear."

And so it went for hours or days, John Malcolm knew not which. The voice described an ancestor, a happy quality and shivered with love. The voice called Calum a treasure, Knut a diamond, Freya a dear daughter.

Over Agtelek, the voice described with awe the ancient animal drawings on the cave walls.

"I love your art, laughter, babies, music, the way you dreamed and built cities and overcame challenges.

That is why I created you.

I love humans by ones and twos, and as a race. At creation, I gave you gifts that I gave no other creatures. Among those gifts was freedom

Sometimes you used your freedom to your hurt.

I could have stopped the whole thing anytime, you know. With just a word.

I considered it.

Then I would think of Adda, that wonderful man who almost crossed from Africa to Europe. Adda, who lived with scarcity, hunted, fed his clan, reproduced so your species would continue. Old Adda, who did not get everything he wanted. But he loved life and fought hard for it.

I too am a fighter. I had my cuts and bruises. Took my chances.

You know the story of Golgotha.

You know also that before I paid the price to put all things right, I cherished life. Ate and drank. My first miracle was making wine from water. For a wedding!

I loved my friends.

Even better,

I liked them.

Peter, John, Mary Magdalene. What times we had together!

Do you find it strange, John Malcolm, that the God of the universe likes you?"

John lay back and looked at the starry heavens. To be on this side, healed, whole, reunited with his loved ones, was a wonder. To understand the best was always yet to be, forever, was intoxicatingly delicious.

John Malcolm did not answer. The beauty of full acceptance and love rolled over him as a mighty ocean, underneath, around, within.

"We could not have *this*, John Malcolm,

If we had not gone through *that*,

Together."

John feels himself gently returned to his place of sleep.

It was a night of wonder.

Some of it,

He understood.

WORSHIP

The worship of God is continuous and everywhere in Heaven. Sometimes the worship is with hands, baking bread. Other times, the worshiper builds a chair or turns a potter's wheel.

Worship of the Maker is with friends over dinner, and alone under forest canopy.

At Al Amin, worship is weaving carpets and praying over them as they are completed.

In Heaven's Great City, worship is collective, congregational. Voices join to sing the old songs, repeat sacred words. Ears collectively hear God's voice, the music of his love.

John enters from the back, with Gloria and Emilie. He moves slowly into the crowd, to the middle. He finds a place where they can see and hear.

"Hear Oh Israel, the Lord our God, the Lord is One."

The congregation repeats the sacred words. John looks to the left to see Adda with his band, who lived before Israel existed or those words were spoken. Adda echoes the *Shema Israel* with special vehemence. Adda's wives, with Yar and Ob, raise their hands and repeat, "The Lord is One."

Ruk and his people are to John's left, swarthy and muscular. John's eyes meet Ruk's and they smile at each other. It is always this way when an ancestor meets a child for the first time.

Only three rows forward, Freya sits with her arm around Lilla.

The congregation says together,

"Christ is Risen."

And repeats as one,

"He is risen indeed!"

Freya turns to see John and silently mouths, "Valkommen."

She nudges Lilla who sees John and smiles. Lilla taps the man on her left, and Knut turns. He motions John, Gloria and Emilie forward and clears space for them next to his family.

He leans over and whispers in John's ear, "There are many here who wish to meet you.

There is Calum, the Scottish sea captain and Lars, the soldier. They are at the front.

A Hungarian Count and a Communist, inseparable friends, heard about your arrival.

So did two Indian traffic cops. They are on bed rest."

Knut and John chuckle.

Someone at the front starts an old hymn and the congregation joins in. John Malcolm reaches a hand for Gloria's on his left and Knut's on his right. The entire congregation stand to their feet and raise hands singing,

"Through many dangers, toils and snares,
We have already come,
Twas grace that brought us safe thus far
And Grace that brought us home.

When we've been here ten thousand years,
bright shining as the sun,
We've no less days to sing God's praise,
than when we first begun."

John, a newcomer to the City, is overwhelmed to see redeemed millions, four and twenty elders, Isaiah's living creatures and a cloud of witnesses, break into praise of the Creator.

Finally, the Spirit of the Lord comes down in cloud and fire as in the days of Israel's sojourn. God's presence is indescribable and God Himself gives the benediction.

Although the benediction is general, John hears it personally.

God can do that.

"John Malcolm,

There will be no more death, nor sorrow, nor crying, neither will there be any more pain:

The former things have passed away.

I am making all things new."

AFTERWORD

These are bad times.

Our ancestors would tell us, if they could, that tough times are normal. We are here because some of them persevered through, long enough to beget others of our ancestors.

Our ancestors would tell is, if they could, that their bad times were a lot worse than anything we have seen. They would challenge us to terrible times matches and win every game.

The most important thing that our ancestors would tell us, is that hard times do not last forever. That is why they did not quit, give up or lay down. God's Heaven is approaching.

It is endless.

John Malcolm was a good man, a little bit angry with God about the loss of his daughter.

God has big shoulders. He can handle our anger.

Maybe John Malcolm is one of the ancestors who would tell us, if he could, that tough times are normal; that God will help us through them, and on the other side there is a place called Heaven.

Where our lives make sense,

We are healed,

And we meet the people we cherish.

This is not just a nice story, if Jesus Christ really did rise from the dead.

See you on the other side, John Malcolm.

Lightning Source UK Ltd.
Milton Keynes UK
UKHW041850261020
372285UK00001B/90